ASCONIUS
PEDIANUS, QUINTUS
Commentaries on Five Speeches
of Cicero

Edited with a Translation by
Simon Squires

Published by
BRISTOL CLASSICAL PRESS (U.K.)
General Editor: John H. Betts

and

BOLCHAZY-CARDUCCI PUBLISHERS (U.S.A.)

Editorial matter © Simon Squires, 1990

Printed in the United States of America

Library of Congress Catalog Number:
90-80780

U.K.	U.S.A.
BRISTOL CLASSICAL PRESS	**BOLCHAZY-CARDUCCI PUBLISHERS**
226 North Street	1000 Brown Street
Bedminster	Unit 101
Bristol BS3 1JD	Wauconda, IL 60084
ISBN 1-85399-051-5	ISBN 0-86516-220-4

A CIP Catalogue record for this book is available from the British Library

CONTENTS

TRANSLATOR'S PREFACE

This book has no special pretensions and makes no claims to originality: its main purpose is to translate what remains of the work of Quintus Asconius Pedianus, and so to make him more accessible to those who study the history of the late Roman Republic without much knowledge of the Latin language. I have therefore tried above all to reflect his meaning as closely as possible, without imposing on him an elegance which his writing often does not possess; and since his regular procedure is to attach his comments to short quotations from the speech of Cicero he is discussing, it seemed helpful to try to reflect the contrast between the styles of the two men, by generally making elegance more apparent in the quotations from Cicero than in his commentator's writing.

The *Oxford Classical Text* of A. C. Clark (1907) has been printed on the left-hand pages in this book; where that text is fragmentary or has been marked by Clark with an *obelus* (†), I have made some attempt in my translation to produce sense, except where the state of the text rendered that a hopeless task. Such areas of doubt are indicated in the translation by question marks if some sense is recoverable, by square brackets in the case of an actual gap in the text, and by dots in cases of complete desperation. Like Clark, I have preserved the sequence of speeches shown in the manuscripts, illogical though it is, instead of adopting a chronological order.

Certain other features which need explanation are as follows:

1. At those points where Clark's *Oxford Classical Text* begins a new page, I have inserted (in both Latin text and translation) that page number, printed in bold italics, in parentheses, thus: *(2)*.

2. If the speech of Cicero being discussed by Asconius survives independently of him, Clark prefaces each quotation in his Latin text with the section reference number normally used in editions of Cicero. These figures are reproduced also in this translation, and are printed in roman typeface, inside square brackets, thus: [§4].

3. Where Asconius identifies a year by giving the names
of the two consuls for that year, I have shown the date
according to our conventional numeration, in light italics,
thus: *58 B.C.* In addition, events to which Asconius refers
without giving the consular year have been similarly
dated numerically where this is possible.

4. Pages in this book are identified throughout in cross-
references as (e.g.) "A. p. 103".

A problem familiar to any translator dealing with
Roman institutions is that certain words or phrases have
no exact equivalent in English, or that in some cases the
equivalent commonly used can be actually misleading: for
example, it is not helpful to anyone to talk of the *equites*
in the late Republic as "horsemen" or even "knights" –
and it seems impossibly clumsy to speak of "gentlemen
outside the senate" (as adopted by one translator of
Cicero's speeches) at every occurrence. Instead I have
adopted the practice of some translations in the LACTOR
series and left certain terms untranslated, in italics (as
for instance *equites*, *tribuni aerarii*), and gathered them
together in a Glossary at the end, where their implica-
tions can be briefly discussed.

Proper names are normally printed in the translation
as they appear in Asconius' text; but I have made an
exception of Cn. Pompeius Magnus, the consul of 70, 55,
and 52 B.C.: to avoid confusion with various other
Pompeiuses, I have always called him "Pompey", and used
"Pompeius" to refer to all other persons bearing that
name. Furthermore, I have taken one significant liberty in
my translation (while leaving Clark's text unaltered): this
has been to redesignate Sex. *Clodius* as Sex. *Cloelius*,
following the widely accepted arguments of D. R. Shackleton Bailey (*Classical Quarterly* 1960, pp. 41 f.). Here again,
the aim is to avoid confusing the reader who might
otherwise be encouraged to draw false inferences.

I have tried to keep footnotes to the minimum (there
is surely something macabre about a commentary on a
commentary). Those which I have included are provided
solely to explain a point in Asconius' work which would
otherwise be baffling, and which could not be dealt with
by simply inserting a parenthesis in the translation. They
do not attempt to follow up the major topics of Roman
History.

There is good reason for thinking that Asconius' *Commentary* was once rather longer than the text which has survived. It was the scholar Poggio Bracciolini who in 1416 discovered a text of Asconius at St Gallen (in modern Switzerland), languishing in a "murky and filthy prison unfit even for condemned murderers"; on 15 December he wrote to Guarinus of Verona about his discovery, and referred to a commentary by Asconius on *eight* speeches of Cicero. Furthermore, in several places Asconius himself inserts a cross-reference into his work ("as I have already mentioned") which cannot be correlated with any passage in the surviving text. These remarks have been reproduced in this translation with the sign "≠" attached. There are also places where Asconius' statements can be shown to be simply incorrect: they have been translated as they occur, and a list of the main demonstrable errors is given in an Appendix (p. 152).

During the preparation of this book I have had much generous assistance from Mr Jeremy Paterson, Senior Lecturer in Classics, University of Newcastle upon Tyne: it was he who suggested in the first place that it would be useful equipment for the student of Late Republican Rome, and he has taken a most helpful interest throughout. In a great many places the book has benefited from his close scrutiny, although it is both conventional and also wholly true to say that he is not to be blamed for those shortcomings which have resulted from my neglect of his advice. I am grateful also to my colleague Mr Tony Griffiths, Senior Classics Master of the Royal Grammar School, Newcastle upon Tyne, for reading my efforts in draft and doing his best to see to it that I never got away with vague or unhelpful writing. And to my wife Ann I am grateful for much sound advice, much tolerance, and the loan of her computer.

Simon Squires
Durham, October 1989

WHO WAS ASCONIUS?

Under the year A.D. 76, the *Chronicle* of Jerome (borrowing from Suetonius, *Lives of famous men*) tells us:

> Q. Asconius Pedianus, distinguished historical writer, became blind at the age of 73 and lived for 12 more years as a universally respected figure.

Generally speaking, it is probably fair to say that the date of a man's death is more likely to be derived from a reliable source than that of an event during his life; so the conclusion should probably be: Born 9 B.C., lost eyesight A.D. 64, died A.D. 76. Two anecdotes reported about Asconius are compatible with this outline:

> (1) The two consuls were Iunius Blaesus and Lucius ⟨Antistius Vetus⟩; Blaesus was invited to the banquet and towed Asconius Pedianus along uninvited like a dinghy . . . Several elderly men including Iunius discussed wrestling there, Iunius being then aged sixty (The *Suda* s.v. Apicius).

> (2) Asconius Pedianus reports hearing Gallus say that this *Eclogue* had been written in his [Gallus'] honour (Servius on Virgil, *Eclogue* 4.11).

The consular year referred to in (1) is A.D. 28; ⟨C. Asinius⟩ Gallus is known to have died in A.D. 33 (Tacitus, *Annals* 6.23). We must presumably discard reluctantly the attractive statement in the Scholiast on Virgil, *Eclogues* 3.106, that Asconius personally heard Virgil speak (Virgil died 19 B.C.).

So much for *when?* The next question is *where?* It is generally agreed that when Asconius calls the historian Livy "our own" (*noster*, A. p. 117) he means that he, like Livy, came from Patavium (modern *Padova*) in northern Italy; since Asconius constantly tells us proudly of his researches in state records like the *Acta* (see Glossary), and discusses in some detail the location of certain buildings at Rome (see e.g. A. pp. 41, 77, 139f.), we can assume that he migrated to Rome at some point in his life, and that he writes at least partly for readers who were like himself provincials.

Indeed it is when Asconius tackles the explanation of a technical point of senatorial procedure (A. p. 69) that the purpose of his *Commentary* becomes more precisely apparent: his sons have not yet reached the age of 25 at which they qualify to attend meetings of the senate, and the procedure needs to be clarified for them. It is therefore very likely that the initial inspiration behind the *Commentary* was a desire to prepare his sons for a career in public life at Rome by enabling them to read the speeches of the most distinguished orator of the Late Republic with proper understanding. The rather didactic and even pedantic manner of Asconius' writing is then easily explained.

The *Commentary* translated in this book was far from being Asconius' only written work: he seems to have composed a *Defence of Virgil against his critics* and a biography of the C. Sallustius who was politically active in the 50s B.C., and who himself wrote the extant *Conspiracy of Catilina* (see Introduction to *In toga candida*, A. p. 125, on the subject of Catilina). Pliny the Elder (*Natural History* 7.159) tells us of a man of 110 whose remarkable age was recorded by Asconius; perhaps we have here a trace of a lost *Essay on long-lived persons*?

A NOTE ON THE SOURCES OF ASCONIUS

[For a full discussion of this topic, and a table of authors specifically mentioned by Asconius, see Marshall, pp. 39ff.]

Asconius is unusual in the ancient world in the frequency with which he mentions explicitly the sources of particular items of information, and in the apparent breadth of his reading. One has to make allowances of course: an ancient writer must have had great physical difficulty in consulting texts in scroll form, and memory will have played a significant part; but the resemblance between his methods and those of modern scholarship has often been noticed. Sometimes, for example, he not only cites the author by name but also gives a reference to the part of the work in question (see A. pp. 19, 75). Sometimes he adjudicates on a disagreement between his sources (A. p. 53). Occasionally, and very interestingly, he reports a search in one or more authors which has *failed* to yield certain information: presumably this means that he has hunted all the way through the writers in

question (see especially A. p. 103).

I add here some short comments on certain individual sources.

1. Cicero. Some of Asconius' comments are clearly deductions based on the text of the speech he is discussing (A. p. 5: explicit reference to *In Pisonem*; p. 51: cf. *Pro Milone* 25). But he had also read and used the *Expositio consiliorum suorum* (A. p. 131), now lost, and some works on oratorical theory (A. pp. 21, 103). Curiously, he seems not to have used the *Letters to Atticus* (the rather inconclusive argument at A. p. 133 could have been omitted on the strength of a quick glance at *ad Att.* 1.1).

2. The *Acta* (see also Glossary s.v.). These are the source most frequently cited, and Asconius claims to have done some thorough research in them (A. p. 69). Five out of the six citations occur in the comments on *Pro Milone*.

3. Fenestella (52 B.C.–A.D. 19?), writer of annalistic Roman history in 22 books. Asconius refers to him five times by name (six? see *In Pisonem* note 1; perhaps even seven? see A. p. 107), nearly always to state a disagreement; a case of academic hostility maybe.

4. Livy. Probably a native of Asconius' home town (see Introduction p. vii above). He is cited just twice by name, which seems surprisingly seldom; Marshall suggests that a debt to Livy lies behind certain unspecific references to familiar information (e.g. A. p. 15 "you realize").

5. Sallustius. Cited once only as an author (A. p. 103, referring to his *Historiae*?). Curiously, Asconius does not admit to using Sallustius' *Conspiracy of Catilina* in his work on *In toga candida*.

SHORT BIBLIOGRAPHY

Text of Asconius:
ed. A. Kiessling-R. Schöll, Berlin 1875
ed. A. C. Clark, *Oxford Classical Text*, Oxford 1907

Text, including comments on Cicero's speeches by other authors:
Scholiastae ed. T. Stangl, Vienna 1912

Full historical commentary:
B. A. Marshall, Missouri 1985

Relevant Cicero speeches:
Pro Milone, ed. A. C. Clark (text and commentary including Asconius), Oxford 1895
In Pisonem, ed. R. G. M. Nisbet (text and commentary), Oxford 1961
Pro Milone, In Pisonem, Pro Scauro, trans. N. H. Watts, Loeb Classical Library 1931
In Catilinam, Pro Milone, trans. M. Grant (*Selected Political Speeches*[2]), Penguin, London 1973

Useful further reading:
Cicero, *Murder Trials*, trans. M. Grant, Penguin, London 1975
Sallust, *The Conspiracy of Catiline*, trans. S. A. Handford, Penguin, London 1963

E. S. Gruen, *The last generation of the Roman Republic*, Berkeley and Los Angeles 1974
A. W. Lintott, *Violence in Republican Rome*, Oxford 1968
H. H. Scullard, *From the Gracchi to Nero*[5], London 1982, chapter VI
Jeremy Paterson, "Politics in the Late Republic" (*Roman Political Life 90 B.C.-A.D. 69*, pp. 21ff., ed. T. P. Wiseman), Exeter 1985
Oxford Classical Dictionary (2nd ed.), Oxford 1970

IN PISONEM

[See R. G. M. Nisbet (ed.) *Cicero, In Pisonem Oratio*, Oxford 1961.]

Cicero's invective against L. Calpurnius Piso Caesoninus, father of Iulius Caesar's wife Calpurnia, survives nearly intact except for the beginning – the quotations concerning Placentia (A. pp. 7f.), for example, are not found anywhere in the principal manuscripts of the speech. Cicero's "masterpiece of misrepresentation" (Nisbet p. xvi) needs to be seen against the background of the formation in late 60 of the so-called "First Triumvirate". (The use of this label is in fact misleading, since the alliance of Iulius Caesar, Pompey, and M. Crassus was not brought into being by legal process, and was not an office of state, unlike for instance that of M. Antonius, M. Lepidus, and the future emperor Augustus, which dominated the struggles of the 30s. Nevertheless, like most other modern writers, I shall use this title for convenience of reference.)

In essence, the First Triumvirate was an electoral pact, not unlike the one which backed Catilina in the elections of 64 (see the *Exposition* to *In Toga Candida*, A. p. 129). It aimed to secure the election of Iulius Caesar as consul for 59, against the bitter opposition of *optimates* such as M. Calpurnius Bibulus; in the pursuit of this objective it naturally sought to attract new supporters and reward existing ones; Cicero himself was at first invited to be included in the clique, although he in fact declined to join.

Then in 58 B.C. P. Clodius Pulcher, *tribunus plebis*, arranged for Cicero's exile by exploiting the dubious legality of Cicero's handling of the conspiracy of Catilina in 63. Clodius' action no doubt was intended to reassert the principle that a Roman citizen could not be put to death without due legal process; but it was also part of a personal vendetta, since Cicero had in 62 undermined Clodius' alibi in the *Bona Dea* trial (in which Clodius was acquitted amid much scandal). Cicero probably hoped that the First Triumvirate would protect him against Clodius, but the legislation passed in 59 B.C. was vulnerable

to attack by Clodius on procedural grounds (as Cicero himself acknowledged in his speech *Pro Sestio* 40; see also Index s.v. Aelius and Fufius), and the Triumvirate remained silent.

Next, Cicero might have expected help from the consuls of 58, Piso and A. Gabinius, since his relations with them had been good, but Clodius secured promising provinces for them, and they too took no action. When Cicero eventually returned to Rome in 57, it was to Pompey that he was indebted – and Pompey by then was once more enjoying close relations with Iulius Caesar in the Triumvirate. So in 56, when the opportunity arose, Cicero could use his speech *De provinciis consularibus* to announce his own good relations with Caesar and to pursue his own personal feud with Piso and Gabinius by proposing their recall from their provinces. (This feud was so bitter that in §96 of the *In Pisonem* Cicero seems almost to exult in the destruction of Piso's army in his province of Macedonia). Now, in 55, Cicero no doubt felt that (as Nisbet puts it, p. xvi) a further attack on Piso "would relieve his feelings and give warning that he was still dangerous". Though the *In Pisonem* is delivered not in a court but before the senate, it takes advantage of an opportunity commonly exploited in the criminal courts: to attack a politician soon after his return to Rome for alleged misconduct as governor of a province.

On the subject of personal feuds see further D. Epstein, *Personal enmity in Roman politics.*

I. IN SENATV CONTRA L. PISONEM

Haec oratio dicta est Cn. Pompeio Magno II M. Crasso II coss. ante paucos dies quam Cn. Pompeius ludos faceret quibus theatrum a se factum dedicavit. Hoc intellegi ex ipsius Ciceronis verbis potest quae in hac oratione posuit. Dixit enim sic: *Instant post hominum memoriam apparatissimi magnificentissimique ludi.* ... quidem posuit hanc inter eas orationes quas dixit Cicero L. Domitio Appio Claudio coss. ultimam. Sed ut ego ab eo dissentiam facit primum quod Piso reversus est ex provincia Pompeio et Crasso consulibus, Gabinius Domitio et Appio: hanc autem orationem dictam ante Gabini reditum ex ipsa manifestum est. Deinde magis quidem naturale est ut Piso recenti reditu invectus sit in Ciceronem responderitque insectationi eius qua revocatus erat ex provincia quam post anni intervallum. Apparet autem Ciceronem respondisse Pisoni. In summa, cum dicat in ipsa oratione Cicero instare magnificentissimos apparatissimosque ludos, non video quo modo hoc magis Domitio et Appio coss. dictum sit, quibus consulibus nulli notabiliores *(2)* ludi fuerunt, quam Pompeio et Crasso, quo anno Pompeius exquisitissimis magnificentissimisque omnis generis ludis theatrum dedicavit.

Argumentum orationis huius breve admodum est. Nam cum revocati essent ex provinciis Piso et Gabinius sententia Ciceronis quam dixerat de provinciis consularibus Lentulo et Philippo consulibus, reversus in civitatem Piso de insectatione Ciceronis in senatu conquestus est et in eum invectus, fiducia maxime Caesaris generi qui tum Gallias obtinebat. Pisoni Cicero respondit hac oratione.

E N A R R A T I O

CIRCA VERS. A PRIMO ✳✳✳

Quod minimum specimen in te ingeni? Ingeni autem?

I. *Speech delivered to the senate against L. Piso*

This speech was delivered in the year when Pompey and M. Crassus were consuls for the second time *(55 B.C.)*, a few days before Pompey was to hold the games with which he inaugurated the theatre that he had built. This can be discovered from the words that Cicero himself put into his speech, namely: [§65] "The most lavish and splendid games of all time are about to begin . . .". Now admittedly [. . .]¹ places the speech last of those that Cicero delivered in the consulship of L. Domitius and Appius Claudius *(54 B.C.)*. What forces me to disagree with him is first the fact that Piso returned from his province when Pompey and Crassus were consuls, while Gabinius did so in the consulship of Domitius and Appius; and clearly this speech was delivered before Gabinius came home. Secondly, Piso would more naturally have attacked Cicero soon after his return (and replied to the harassment which had led to his recall) rather than after a year had passed. And it seems that Cicero did respond to Piso's rhetoric. In brief, when Cicero says in this speech that "the most lavish and splendid games are about to begin", it is much more likely that they took place in Pompey and Crassus' consulship, when Pompey dedicated his theatre with the most lavish and exquisite games possible, than during the year of Domitius and Appius, *(2)* when there were no particularly noteworthy games.

The exposition of this speech can be stated quite briefly: Piso and Gabinius were recalled from their provinces on the proposal of Cicero, which was made in his "Speech on the consuls' provinces", delivered in the consulship of Lentulus and Philippus *(56 B.C.)*; on his return Piso complained in the senate about Cicero's persecution of him, and then launched his attack on Cicero, relying particularly on his son-in-law, Caesar, who was then in command of the provinces of Gaul.² In the present speech Cicero made his response to Piso.

C O M M E N T A R Y

(about [. . .] lines from the start)

Is there in you the smallest sign of talent? Did I say

immo ingenui hominis ac liberi: qui colore ipso patriam aspernaris, oratione genus, moribus nomen.

Tametsi haec oratio sic inscribitur: *In L. Pisonem*; tamen non puto vos ignorare hunc Pisonem ex ea familia esse quae Frugi appellata sit: et ideo dicit aspernari eum moribus nomen.

CIRCA VERS. LXXX

Hoc non ad contemnendam Placentiam pertinet unde se is ortum gloriari solet: neque enim hoc mea natura fert, nec municipi, praesertim de me optime meriti, dignitas patitur.

Magnopere me haesitare confiteor quid sit qua re Cicero *(3)* Placentiam municipium esse dicat. Video enim in annalibus eorum qui Punicum bellum secundum scripserunt tradi Placentiam coloniam deductam pridie Kal. Iun. primo anno eius belli, P. Cornelio Scipione, patre Africani prioris, Ti. Sempronio Longo coss. Neque illud dici potest, sic eam coloniam esse deductam quemadmodum post plures aetates Cn. Pompeius Strabo, pater Cn. Pompei Magni, Transpadanas colonias deduxerit. Pompeius enim non novis colonis eas constituit sed veteribus incolis manentibus ius dedit Latii, ut possent habere ius quod ceterae Latinae coloniae, id est ut petendo magistratus civitatem Romanam adipiscerentur. Placentiam autem sex milia hominum novi coloni deducti sunt, in quibus equites ducenti. Deducendi fuit causa ut opponerentur Gallis qui eam partem Italiae tenebant. Deduxerunt III viri P. Cornelius Asina, P. Papirius Maso, Cn. Cornelius Scipio. Eamque coloniam LIII . . . deductam esse invenimus: deducta est autem Latina. Duo porro genera earum coloniarum quae a populo Romano deductae sunt fuerunt, ut Quiritium aliae, aliae Latinorum essent. De se autem optime meritos Placentinos ait, quod illi quoque honoratissima decreta erga Ciceronem fecerunt certaveruntque in ea re cum tota Italia, cum de reditu eius actum est. *(4)*

PAVLO POST

De avo Pisonis materno:

Hic cum a domo profectus Placentiae forte consedisset paucis post annis in eam civitatem – nam tum erat . . . – ascendit. Prius enim Gallus, dein Gallicanus, extremo

talent? I should rather have said a sign of a gentlemanly and free-born man, since by your complexion you throw contempt on your country, on your family by your speech, and on your name by your habits.

Though this speech is labelled "against L. Piso", you are doubtless aware that this Piso was from the family named "Thrifty";[3] this is why he says that he throws contempt on his name by his habits.

(about line 80)

This does not contribute towards making us despise Placentia, which is the origin he boasts of: that is not my way, and the distinction of that municipium, *which has done me great service, does not permit that conclusion.*

I must admit that I am not at all clear why Cicero calls Placentia a *municipium*. *(3)* In the annals of those who have compiled the history of the Second Punic War I see Placentia listed as a *colonia*, installed on 31 May in the first year of that war *(218 B.C.)* (the consulship of Ti. Sempronius Longus and P. Cornelius Scipio, father of the elder Africanus). Furthermore, it cannot be argued that the *colonia* was installed in the manner adopted much later on north of the river Po by Cn. Pompeius Strabo, father of Pompey; in that instance Pompeius did not inaugurate them with fresh colonists, but gave to existing inhabitants the "Latin rights" enjoyed by other Latin *coloniae*, that of access to Roman citizenship by securing local political office. Now Placentia received 6000 fresh colonists, including 200 *equites*; the purpose of settling them there was that they should resist the Gauls who were occupying that part of Italy. The leaders were three men: P. Cornelius Asina, P. Papirius Maso, and Cn. Cornelius Scipio; and we notice that 53 [. . .] installed, but it was a Latin settlement. Furthermore, there were two types of Roman *colonia*, that of Roman citizens and that of Latins. Cicero says that the Placentines have done him great service because they passed an honorific decree at his restoration from exile, competing in this with the whole of Italy.[4]

(4) (shortly afterwards)
He speaks of Piso's maternal grandfather:
He left home and as it happened settled in Placentia, and after a few years achieved citizenship there, since it was then a [. . .]. First he was regarded as a Gaul, then

Placentinus haberi coeptus est.

Hoc quod dicit civitatem fuisse Placentiam, ab eadem persuasione ponit municipium fuisse. Avum autem maternum Pisonis primo Gallum fuisse ideo ait quod venisse eum in Italiam dicit trans Alpis, dein Gallicanum, quod in Italia consederit, Placentinum denique, postquam adscitus sit a Placentinis. Sed Pisonis avus multo post ea tempora fuit quibus Placentia colonia est deducta.

CIRCA VERS. A PRIMO ✳✳✳

Lautiorem . . . pater tuus socerum quam C. Piso . . . in illo luctu meo. Ei enim filiam meam collocavi quem ego, si mihi potestas tum omnium fuisset, unum potissimum delegissem.

(5) Quis fuerit socer Pisonis patris ipse supra dixit his verbis:

Insuber quidam fuit, idem mercator et praeco: is cum Romam cum filia venisset, adulescentem nobilem, Caesonini hominis furacissimi filium, ausus est appellare, eique filiam collocavit. Calventium aiunt eum appellatum.

Ipsius Pisonis contra quem haec oratio est socerum Rutilium Nudum Fenestella tradit. Cicero filiam post mortem Pisonis generi P. Lentulo collocavit, apud quem illa ex partu decessit.

CIR. VER. A PRIMO CCLXX

[§4] *Ego in C. Rabirio perduellionis reo XXXX annis ante me consulem interpositam senatus auctoritatem sustinui contra invidiam atque defendi.*

Possit aliquis credere errare Ciceronem, quod dicat quadraginta annis factum esse ut ex S.C. arma adversus L. Appuleium Saturninum tribunum plebis sumerentur. C. enim Mario L. Valerio coss. id senatum decrevisse, qui coss. annis ante consulatum Ciceronis XXXVII fuerint. Sed hic non subtilis computatio annorum facta est verum summatim *(6)* tempus comprehensum est, ut proinde debeamus accipere ac si dixerit: *prope XXXX annis.* Haec consuetudo in ipsis orationibus est: itaque Cicero in ea quoque quam habuit in Catilinam in senatu, ait . . . octavus decimus dies esset postea quam factum est senatus consultum ut viderent consules ne quid res publica detrimenti caperet, dixit vicesimum diem habere se

a provincial Gaul, and in the end a Placentine.

Cicero's motive in implying that Placentia was a *civitas* is the same as that which makes him call it a *municipium*. He says that Piso's grandfather was first a Gaul because of having entered Italy across the Alps, then a provincial Gaul because he settled in Italy, and finally a Placentine after the inhabitants co-opted him. But Piso's grandfather lived long after the *colonia* was installed at Placentia.

(about [. . .] lines from the start)

Your father [looked for?] a more polished son-in-law than C. Piso at that time of my grief. For I betrothed my daughter to the one man I should have chosen if I had had an entirely unlimited choice.

(5) Cicero describes the man who was the father-in-law of Piso's father in these words:

There was a certain Insubrian, a merchant and auctioneer, who came to Rome with his daughter; he actually described a nobilis *young man as the son of a thieving creature called Caesoninus, and betrothed his daughter to him. His name is alleged to have been Calventius.*

According to Fenestella the name of the father-in-law of our Piso was Rutilius Nudus. After the death of Piso the son-in-law, Cicero betrothed his daughter to P. Lentulus,[5] and she later died in childbirth.

(about 270 lines from the start)

[§4] *The senate's authority was exerted 40 years before my consulship, and I upheld and defended that authority against its critics at the trial of C. Rabirius for* perduellio *(63 B.C.).*

It might be thought that Cicero is mistaken in saying that 40 years beforehand force had been authorized by decree of the senate against the *tribunus plebis* L. Appuleius Saturninus; for the decree was dated in the year of the consuls C. Marius and L. Valerius *(100 B.C.)*, 37 years before Cicero's own consulship. But here we have a not absolutely precise reckoning of years: *(6)* in effect he might have said "about 40 years". In fact Cicero has this habit in his speeches, as in the speech against Catilina in the senate *(63 B.C.)*;[6] the truth was that it was now the eighteenth day since the passing of the decree which instructed the consuls to protect the state from

S.C. tamquam in vagina reconditum.

CIR. VERS. A PRIMO CCC

[§6] *Ego cum in contione abiens magistratu dicere a tribuno plebis prohiberer quae constitueram, cum is mihi tantum modo iurare permitteret, sine ulla dubitatione iuravi rem p. atque hanc urbem mea unius opera esse salvam.*

Diximus iam antea a Q. Metello Nepote tr.pl. Ciceronem consulatu abeuntem prohibitum esse contionari de rebus quas in eo magistratu gessit.

CIR. VER. A PRIMO CCCXX

Dicit de ludis Compitaliciis:

[§8] *Quos Q. Metellus – facio iniuriam fortissimo (7) viro mortuo, qui illum cuius paucos pares haec civitas tulit cum hac importuna belua conferam –, sed ille designatus consul, cum quidam tr.pl. suo auxilio magistros ludos contra S.C. facere iussisset, privatus fieri vetuit. – Tu cum in Kal. Ian. Compitaliorum dies incidisset, Sex. Clodium, qui numquam ante praetextatus fuisset, ludos facere et praetextatum volitare passus es.*

L. Iulio C. Marcio consulibus quos et ipse Cicero supra memoravit senatus consulto collegia sublata sunt quae adversus rem publicam videbantur esse constituta. Solebant autem magistri collegiorum ludos facere, sicut magistri vicorum faciebant, Compitalicios praetextati, qui ludi sublatis collegiis discussi sunt. Post VI deinde annos quam sublata erant P. Clodius tr.pl. lege lata restituit collegia. Invidiam ergo et crimen restitutorum confert in Pisonem, quod, cum consul esset, passus sit ante quam lex ferretur facere Kal. Ianuar. praetextatum ludos Sex. Clodium. Is fuit familiarissimus Clodii et operarum Clodianarum dux, quo auctore postea illato ab eis corpore Clodii curia cum eo incensa est. Quos ludos tunc quoque fieri prohibere temptavit L. Ninnius tr.pl. Ante biennium autem quam restituerentur collegia, Q. Metellus Celer consul designatus magistros vicorum ludos Compitalicios

harm,[7] but he actually said that the decree had been
kept "so to speak in its sheath" for twenty days.

(about 300 lines from the start)
[§6] *When I was laying down my office I was prevented
by a tribunus plebis from saying what I intended, and he
allowed me simply to swear the oath; without hesitation I
swore that by my efforts alone the state and this city
was intact.*

    I have already noted (≠) that at the end of his term
of office Cicero was prevented by the *tribunus plebis* Q.
Metellus Nepos from addressing the public on his achieve-
ments during that term.

(about 320 lines from the start)
Cicero refers to the Compitalician Games:
[§8] *When Q. Metellus was consul-elect – I do an injustice
to a courageous man (7) now dead and a rare citizen in
comparing him to this appalling savage – (but to resume)
a tribunus plebis by his own prerogative ordered the
masters of the Games to celebrate them despite a senatorial decree, and Q. Metellus though a private citizen
forbade this. Now when the Compitalicia fell on 1 January,
you allowed Sex. Cloelius,[8] who had never yet worn the
toga of office, to hold the Games and prance about in his
robes.*

    In the consulship of L. Iulius and C. Marcius *(64
B.C.)*, whom Cicero mentions earlier, a decree of the
senate abolished the *collegia* as being contrary to the
public interest. The masters of these *collegia* were in the
habit of wearing the toga of office when holding the
Compitalician Games, just like the leaders of the *vici*, with
the abolition of the *collegia* the Games came to an end. Six
years after the abolition the *tribunus plebis* P. Clodius
reintroduced them by legislation *(58 B.C.)*. So Cicero
attributes the blame for this restoration to Piso, who as
consul allowed Sex. Cloelius to wear his official toga to
hold the games on 1 January before the law came into
force. This Cloelius was an intimate of P. Clodius and the
leader of his gang; later on it was at his suggestion that
the body of P. Clodius was carried into the senate-house
and the building set on fire. On the occasion referred to
by Cicero the *tribunus plebis* L. Ninnius tried to stop the
Games. Two years before the *collegia* were reintroduced,
the consul-elect Q. Metellus Celer had stopped the leaders

facere prohibuerat, ut Cicero tradit, quamvis auctore
tribuno plebis fierent ludi; cuius tribuni nomen adhuc non
inveni.

(8) PAVLO POST

[§9] *Ergo his fundamentis positis consulatus tui, triduo*
post, inspectante te et tacente, a fatali portento prodi-
gioque rei publicae lex Aelia et Fufia eversa est, pro-
pugnacula murique tranquillitatis atque oti; collegia non
ea solum quae senatus sustulerat restituta, sed innume-
rabilia quaedam ex omni faece urbis ac servitio concitata.
Ab eodem homine in stupris inauditis nefariisque versato
vetus illa magistra pudoris et modestiae censura sublata
est.

    Diximus L. Pisone A. Gabinio coss. P. Clodium tr.pl.
quattuor leges perniciosas populo Romano tulisse:
annonariam, de qua Cicero mentionem hoc loco non facit –
fuit enim summe popularis – ut frumentum populo quod
antea senis aeris ac trientibus in singulos modios dabatur
gratis daretur: alteram ne quis per eos dies quibus cum
populo agi liceret de caelo servaret; propter quam
rogationem ait legem Aeliam et Fufiam, propugnacula et
muros tranquillitatis atque otii, eversam esse; – obnun-
tiatio enim qua perniciosis legibus resistebatur, quam
Aelia lex confirmaverat, erat sublata –: tertiam de collegiis
restituendis novisque instituendis, quae ait ex servitiorum
faece constituta: quartam ne quem censores in senatu
legendo praeterirent, neve qua ignominia afficerent, nisi
qui apud eos accusatus et utriusque censoris sententia
damnatus esset.

    Hac ergo *(9)* eius lege censuram, quae magistra
pudoris et modestiae est, sublatam ait.

PAVLO POST

[§11] *Persequere continentis his funeribus dies. Pro*
Aurelio tribunali ne conivente quidem te, quod ipsum
esset scelus, sed etiam hilarioribus oculis quam solitus

of *vici* holding the Compitalician Games even though they were being held on the initiative of a *tribunus plebis*, as Cicero tells us; the identity of the *tribunus plebis* is so far unknown to me.[9]

(8) (shortly afterwards)
[§9] *This then was the foundation of your consulship; and three days later, as you looked on in silence, that monster in our state overturned the law of Aelius and Fufius, the rampart and bulwark of our peace and security. Not only were the* collegia *which had been abolished by the senate restored, but countless others were conjured up from the sediment of the city's slave-body. And that same man, practised in unparalleled and villainous debauchery, also abolished the* censura, *that time-honoured governess of decency and restraint.*

We have said (≠) that when L. Piso and A. Gabinius were consuls *(58 B.C.)* the *tribunus plebis* P. Clodius passed four laws damaging to the Roman *populus*: a corn law, not referred to here by Cicero (since it was extremely *popularis*), which enacted that corn should be given free to the *populus* instead of at the price of $6\frac{1}{3}$ *asses* per *modius* charged previously; a second that forbade "watching of the sky" on those days when the *populus'* business could be conducted (this is why Cicero says that the law of Aelius and Fufius, the rampart and bulwark of peace and security, has been overturned; Clodius had abolished the proclamation of ill omens, which was used to obstruct damaging legislation and had been ratified by Aelius' law).[10] The third bill reintroduced *collegia* and formed new ones, which Cicero says have been conjured up from the sediment of the city's slave-body; the fourth laid down that the *censores* should omit no-one in reviewing the senate, and prescribe dishonour for no-one unless he was accused in their presence and condemned by both *censores* together. *(9)* So Cicero says that the *censura*, the time-honoured governess of decency and restraint, has been abolished.

(shortly afterwards)
[§11] *Review if you will the days that followed these funeral rituals. Before the tribunal of Aurelius you did not even avert your gaze – and that would have been a crime in itself - no, you looked on with eyes more joyful*

eras intuente, dilectus servorum habebatur ab eo qui nihil sibi umquam nec facere nec pati turpe duxit.

Profecto intellegitis P. Clodium significari.

CIR. VER. A PRIMO DC

Dicit de Castoris templo:
[§23] *Id autem templum sublato aditu, revolsis gradibus, a coniuratorum reliquiis atque a Catilinae praevaricatore quondam, tum ultore, armis teneretur.*

Catilinam lege repetundarum absolutum esse accusante P. Clodio iam supra dictum est.

STATIM

Cum equites Romani relegarentur, viri boni lapidibus e foro pellerentur.

L. Lamiam a Gabinio consule edicto relegatum esse iam diximus.

(10) CIR. VER. A PRIMO DCXX

[§24] *Seplasia me hercule, te ut primum aspexit, Campanum consulem repudiavit.*

Dictum est in dissuasione legis agrariae apud populum plateam esse Capuae quae Seplasia appellatur, in qua unguentarii negotiari sint soliti. Ergo eos quoque qui in ea platea negotiarentur dicit invitos Pisonem vidisse, cum Capuam consul venit, quod eos a quibus ipse expulsus erat adiuvisset.

CIR. VER. A PRIMO DCXL

[§26] *Ecquod in hac urbe maius umquam incendium fuit cui non consul subveniret? At tu illo ipso tempore apud socrum tuam cuius domum ad meam exhauriendam patefeceras sedebas.*

Post profectionem ex urbe Ciceronis bona eius P. Clodius publicavit; postquam direpta sunt omnia quae aut in domo aut in villis fuerunt, et ex eis ad ipsos consules lata complura, domus direpta primum, deinde inflammata ac diruta est. Socrus Pisonis quae fuerit invenire non potui, videlicet quod auctores rerum non perinde in domibus ac

than usual, as slaves were conscripted by a man who never considered any act or experience degrading to him.
Of course you realize the reference is to P. Clodius.

(about 600 lines from the start)
He says of the temple of Castor:
[§23] *But that temple, with its entrance removed and its steps torn up, was occupied forcibly by the remnant of the conspirators and the man who was once the colluding prosecutor of Catilina and now his avenger.*
I have already mentioned[11] that Catilina was prosecuted by P. Clodius under the law of *res repetundae* and acquitted.

(immediately afterwards)
When Roman equites were being banished and patriots driven from the forum with stones.
We have already said (≠) that L. Lamia was deported by a decree of the consul Gabinius.

(10) (about 620 lines from the start)
[§24] *Indeed as soon as Seplasia set eyes on you it rejected you as a Campanian consul.*
In the speech before the *populus* against the Agrarian Law[12] it is stated that there is in Capua a square called Seplasia, where dealers in ointments do business. So Cicero is saying that the dealers in the square also noticed Piso's arrival in Capua as consul without enthusiasm because he had assisted those by whom he, Cicero, had himself been banished.

(about 640 lines from the start)
[§26] *Has there ever been a serious conflagration in this city without the consul coming to the rescue? Yet at that time you were sitting in the house of your mother-in-law, which you had thrown open to receive the contents of mine.*
After Cicero's departure from Rome, P. Clodius confiscated his property; the entire contents of his house and other residences were seized, and a good deal of them were taken to the consuls; the house was then ransacked, set on fire, and destroyed. I have not managed to find out the name of Piso's mother-in-law, no doubt because while historians transmit to us the names of men, they tend not to do the same with those of women

familiis feminarum, nisi illustrium, ac virorum nomina tradiderunt.

(11) PAVLO POST

[§27] *Ac ne tum quidem emersisti, lutulente Caesonine, e miserrimis naturae sordibus cum experrecta tandem virtus celeriter et verum amicum et optime meritum civem et suum pristinum morem requisivit.*

Profecto Cn. Pompeium significari intellegitis.

CIR. VER. A PRIMO DCCC

[§35] *De me cum omnes magistratus promulgassent praeter unum praetorem a quo non fuit postulandum, fratrem inimici mei, praeterque duos de lapide emptos tribunos, legem comitiis centuriatis tulit P. Lentulus consul.*

Frater ille inimici mei, id est P. Clodi. Ap. Claudius, sicut iam saepe significavi, tum fuit praetor. Duos tribunos de quibus ipsis quoque iam diximus, quos de lapide emptos ait, quia mercede id faciebant, Sex. Atilium Serranum et Q. Numerium significat.

CIR. MEDIVM

[§§38, 39] *Appellatus est hic volturius illius provinciae, si dis placet, imperator. Ne tum quidem, Paule noster, tabellas cum laurea Romam mittere audebas?*

(12) Confido vos intellegere L. Paulum hunc significari qui fuit pater naturalis Africani posterioris, de Macedoniaque ultimum et Perse rege triumphavit. Macedoniam autem Piso in quem haec oratio est obtinuit; propter quod Paulum eum appellat, irridens eum quod ibi rem non prospere gessit.

CIR. MEDIVM

[§44] *M. Marcellus qui ter consul fuit summa virtute, pietate, gloria militari, periit in mari: qui tamen ob virtutem in gloria et laude vivit.*

Fortasse quaeratis quem dicat Marcellum. Fuit autem nepos M. Marcelli eius qui bello Punico secundo Syracusas vicit et quinque consulatus adeptus est. Hic autem Marcellus de quo Cicero dicit naufragio ad ipsam Africam

in their houses and *familiae,* unless they are really distinguished.

(11) (shortly afterwards)
[§27] *And furthermore, you squalid Caesoninus, not even then did you clamber out of your typically pitiful state of degradation, when courage, finally aroused, called urgently for a true friend, for a staunch citizen, for proper principles.*

You realize of course that Pompey is implied.

(about 800 lines from the start)
[§35] *When the bill in my favour had been published by all the magistrates except for one praetor, the brother of my enemy, from whom I could hardly expect such a thing, and except for two* tribuni plebis, *who had been purchased at the auction-stall, that bill was put through the* comitia centuriata *by the consul P. Lentulus.*

He says "the brother of my enemy", the enemy being P. Clodius. I have often mentioned (≠) that Ap. Claudius was then *(57 B.C.)* a praetor. The two *tribuni plebis* whom I have also mentioned already (≠), and who were "purchased at the auction-stall" since they were paid for the service, are Sex. Atilius Serranus and Q. Numerius.

(about half way)
[§§38, 39] *This carrion-crow of that province was hailed, if you please, as General. And did you not venture even then, my dear Paulus, to submit victory dispatches to Rome?*
(12) I am sure you realize that this L. Paulus was the natural father of the younger (Scipio) Africanus, and that his last triumph was over Macedonia and King Perses. Piso himself was governor of Macedonia, and so Cicero calls him "Paulus" to mock his lack of success there.

(about half way)
[§44] *M. Marcellus, a man of the greatest courage, loyalty, and distinction, who was three times consul, died at sea; yet because of his courage he survives in his distinction and reputation.*

You may be wondering which Marcellus he is speaking of. There was a grandson of the M. Marcellus who defeated Syracuse in the Second Punic War and was consul five times. But the Marcellus that Cicero is

periit paulo ante coeptum bellum Punicum tertium. Idem cum statuas sibi ac patri itemque avo poneret in monumentis avi sui ad Honoris et Virtutis, decore subscripsit: *III MARCELLI NOVIES COSS.* Fuit enim ipse ter consul, avus quinquies, pater semel: itaque neque mentitus est et apud imperitiores patris sui splendorem auxit.

CIR. VER. A NOV. DCCCC

[§52] *Me consequentibus diebus in ea ipsa domo qua tu me expuleras, quam incenderas, (13) pontifices, consules, patres conscripti conlocarunt, mihique, quod antea nemini, pecunia publica aedificandam domum censuerunt.*

Hoc Cicero oratorio more, non historico, videtur posuisse: nam multis aetatibus ante Ciceronem nulli id contigisse verum est, nemini vero umquam antea videamus ne parum caute dicat.

Antiquis enim temporibus pluribus idem contigit; nam M. Valerio Maximo, ut Antias tradidit, inter alios honores domus quoque publice aedificata est in Palatio, cuius exitus quo magis insignis esset in publicum versus declinaretur, hoc est, extra privatum aperiretur. Varronem autem tradere M. Valerio, quia Sabinos vicerat, aedes in Palatio tributas, Iulius Hyginus dicit in libro priore de viris claris, et P. Valerio Volesi filio Publicolae aedium publice locum sub Veliis, ubi nunc aedis Victoriae est, populum ex lege quam ipse tulerat concessisse. Tradunt et Antiochi regis filio obsidi domum publice aedificatam, inter quos Atticus in annali: quae postea dicitur Lucili poetae fuisse. Varro quoque in libro III de vita populi Romani, quo loco refert quam gratus fuerit erga bene meritos, dicit Mutinae, quod in Sicilia cum equitatu suo transierat ad nos, civitatem Romae datam aedesque et pecuniam ex aerario.

Videamus tamen num ideo Cicero dicat sibi, quod antea nulli, domum pecunia publica ex aerario aedificatam, quia illis aut locus publice datus sit, aut domus quae non fuerant eorum propter illos publico sumptu aedificatae: Ciceroni domus quae *(14)* fuerat ipsius et diruta atque incensa erat et consecrata publico sumptu aedificata sit:

referring to perished in a shipwreck off Africa shortly before the outbreak of the Third Punic War. When he was erecting statues for his father, his grandfather, and for himself, he added a very suitable inscription on the monument of his grandfather near the shrine of Honor and Virtus: *THREE MARCELLI, NINE TIMES CONSULS.* He was consul himself three times, his grandfather five times, and his father once; so the inscription was quite correct, and increased his father's reputation with those who did not understand the implication.

(about 900 lines from the end)
[§52] *In the succeeding days priests, consuls, and senators installed me in the very house from which you had driven me, which you had set on fire, (13) and resolved that the house should be rebuilt for me at public expense, a quite unprecedented decision.*

Cicero appears to be offering oratory and not history: it is quite true that this honour was conferred on no-one for a very long time before Cicero, but it is somewhat hasty to say that it is unprecedented. In early times there were several cases: Antias tells us that a house was built in the Palatium at public expense, among other honours, for M. Valerius Maximus; and the doors were made to swing outwards into the street, an extra touch of magnificence. Iulius Hyginus says in his first book on famous men that Varro passed to M. Valerius a house in the Palatium as a reward for conquering the Sabines; and that the *populus* granted to P. Valerius Publicola son of Volesus, under his own law, the site for a house below the Velia where the temple of Victory is now, and at public cost. Certain authors, among them Atticus in his *Annals*, tell us that a house was built at public expense for the son of King Antiochus when kept as a hostage; this, they say, later belonged to the poet Lucilius. And Varro again says in his third book "On the way of life of the Roman *populus*" (in a passage concerned with their gratitude towards acts of loyalty) that Mutina was rewarded with Roman citizenship, a house, and money from the treasury for having come over to our side with his cavalry in Sicily. However, we ought to see whether Cicero makes this statement because no-one had previously had a house built with public funds from the treasury - perhaps in the other cases it was the site that was awarded, or else the houses were not their own, but put

quod novum et huic primo et adhuc etiam soli contigit.

CIR. VER. A NOVIS. DCCCXX

[§58] *O stultos Camillos, Curios, Fabricios, Calatinos, Scipiones, Marcellos, Maximos! o amentem Paulum, rusticum Marium, nullius consili patres horum amborum consulum qui triumpharunt!*

Diximus hanc orationem esse dictam Cn. Pompeio Magno II M. Crasso II coss. Pompeii pater bello Italico de Picentibus, M. Crassi pater P. Crassus ante bellum Italicum de Hispanis triumphavit.

CIR. VER. A NOV. DCLX

[§62] *Eadem cupiditate vir summo ingenio praeditus, C. Cotta, nullo certo hoste flagravit. Eorum neuter triumphavit, quod alteri illum honorem collega, alteri mors peremit.*

Credo vos quaerere et quis hic Cotta et quis ille collega Crassi fuerit. Fuit autem C. Cotta orator ille compar P. Sulpici qui est in dialogis Ciceronis de Oratore scriptis. Cum decretus illi esset triumphus, mortuus est ante diem triumphi, cum cicatrix vulneris eius quod ante plures annos in proelio acceperat rescissa esset repente. L. autem Crasso collega fuit Q. Scaevola pontifex qui, cum animadverteret *(15)* Crasso propter summam eius in re publica potentiam ac dignitatem senatum in decernendo triumpho gratificari, non dubitavit rei publicae magis quam collegae habere rationem ac ne fieret S.C. intercessit. Idem provinciam, cuius cupiditate plerique etiam boni viri deliquerant, deposuerat ne sumptui esset †oratio†.

STATIM

[§62] *Inrisa est a te paulo ante M. Pisonis cupiditas triumphandi a qua te longe dixisti abhorrere: qui etiam si minus magnum bellum gesserat, istum honorem omittendum non putavit. Tu eruditior quam Piso.*

Quis hic M. Piso fuerit credo vos ignorare. Fuit autem, ut puto iam nos dixisse, Pupius Piso eisdem temporibus quibus Cicero, sed tanto aetate maior ut

up at public cost on their behalf. *(14)* In Cicero's case his own house was destroyed, burnt, and consecrated, and then rebuilt out of public funds; this was indeed an unique and hitherto unprecedented step.

(about 820 lines from the end)
[§58] *O foolish Camilluses, Curiuses, Fabriciuses, Cala-tinuses, Scipios, Marcelluses, Maximuses! O idiot Paulus, incompetent Marius, how misguided were the fathers of both these consuls – they held triumphs!*

We have said that this speech was delivered during the second consulships of Pompey and M. Crassus, *(55 B.C.)*. Pompey's father triumphed in the Italian War over the Picenes *(89 B.C.)*, and Crassus' father P. Crassus over the Spanish before the Italian War *(93 B.C.)*.

(about 660 lines from the end)
[§62] *That great genius C. Cotta was inspired with the same desire, though without a particular enemy in view; neither triumphed, the one being deprived of the honour by a colleague, the other by death.*

No doubt you are wondering who this Cotta is, and who the colleague of Crassus. C. Cotta as an orator was the equal of P. Sulpicius who features in Cicero's dialogue "On the Orator". He was granted a triumph, but died before the day of the ceremony *(74/3 B.C.)*, since a war-wound suffered some years beforehand suddenly re-opened. The colleague of L. Crassus was the priest Q. Scaevola; he became aware *(15)* that the senate was indulging Crassus by the grant of a triumph because of his enormous power and stature in public life *(95 B.C.)*, so without hesitation he thought of the state rather than of his colleague, and vetoed the proposal in the senate. The desire for a province has even led many *boni* into wrongdoing, but he renounced it so as not to create expense ⟨for the Roman *populus*?⟩.

(immediately afterwards)
[§62] *A little while ago you jeered at M. Piso's desire for a triumph, and claimed you had no such desire; the war he conducted was not significant, yet he did not choose to renounce the honour. You are cleverer than Piso.*

No doubt you are unaware who this M. Piso is. I think I have said before (≠) that it was Pupius Piso, a contemporary of Cicero, but older (Cicero was taken to

adulescentulum Ciceronem pater ad eum deduceret, quod
in eo et antiquae vitae similitudo et multae erant litterae:
orator quoque melior quam frequentior habitus est.
Biennio tamen serius quam Cicero consul fuit; triumphavit
procos. de Hispania Q. Hortensio Q. Metello Cretico coss.
ante Ciceronis consulatum.

PAVLO POST

[§65] *Instant post hominum memoriam apparatissimi
magnificentissimique ludi, quales non (16) modo numquam
fuerunt, sed ne quo modo fieri quidem posthac possint
possum ullo pacto suspicari.*
    Cn. Pompeii ludos significat quibus theatrum a se
factum dedicavit, quibus ludis elephantorum pugnam
primus omnium dedit in Circo.

VER. A NOVIS. DLX

[§68] *Est quidam Graecus qui cum isto vivit, homo, vere
ut dicam – sic enim cognovi – humanus, sed tam diu quam
diu aut cum aliis est aut ipse secum.*
    Philodemum significat qui fuit Epicureus illa aetate
nobilissimus, cuius et poemata sunt lasciva.

CIR. VER. A NOVIS. CCCXX

[§82] *Quamquam, quod ad me attinet,
    numquam istam imminuam curam infitiando tibi.*
    Prope notius est quam ut indicandum sit hunc versum
esse L. Acci poetae et dici a Thyeste Atreo.

CIR. VER. A NOVIS. CC

[§89] *Quod populari illi sacerdoti sescentos ad bestias
socios stipendiariosque misisti.*
    Manifestum est P. Clodium significari.

(17) CIR. VER. A NOVIS. CXX

[§94] *Ecquid vides, ecquid sentis, lege iudiciaria lata,
quos posthac iudices simus habituri?*
    Legem iudiciariam ante aliquot annos quibus
temporibus accusatus est Verres a Cicerone tulit L.
Aurelius Cotta praetor, qua communicata sunt iudicia

see him by his father in his youth, since Piso displayed
an old-fashioned style of life and was highly educated);
as an orator he did not perform often, but was thought
most expert. He became consul two years later than Cicero
(61 B.C.), but triumphed as proconsul over the Spanish
before Cicero's consulship in the year of Q. Hortensius
and Q. Metellus Creticus *(69 B.C.)*.

(shortly afterwards)
[§65] *We are about to celebrate the most splendid and
illustrious games in history: (16) not only are they as yet
unparalleled, but it cannot be supposed that the future
will ever show their equal.*

He means the games held by Pompey to dedicate his
theatre, when he presented the first ever battle of
elephants in the Circus.

(about 560 lines from the end)
[§68] *There is a Greek who lives with him, whom I have
found (to tell the truth) most civilized, as long as he is
with men other than Piso – or is by himself.*

He means Philodemus, a most distinguished Epicurean
of the time; his poems are somewhat risqué.

(about 320 lines from the end)
[§82] *All the same, for my part "I shall not by denial ease
your care".*

This quotation is probably too well-known for me to
need to point out that it is a line by L. Accius the poet,
and is said by Thyestes to Atreus.

(about 200 lines from the end)
[§89] *What of the fact that you sent to that* popularis
*"priest" hosts of friends and allies for dispatch by
beasts?*

Obviously P. Clodius is the person referred to.

(17) (about 120 lines from the end)
[§94] *Do you see, are you aware, what men we are to
have in future as jurors, now that the law on judicial
procedure is passed?*

Such a law was passed by L. Aurelius Cotta, a
praetor, a few years previously *(70 B.C.)*, at the period
when Verres was prosecuted by Cicero; by this law the
juries were to be shared between senators, *equites,* and

senatui et equitibus Romanis et tribunis aerariis. Rursus deinde Pompeius in consulatu secundo, quo haec oratio dicta est promulgavit ut amplissimo ex censu ex centuriis aliter atque antea lecti iudices, aeque tamen ex illis tribus ordinibus, res iudicarent.

CIR. VER. A NOVIS. LXXXX

[§95] *L. Opimius eiectus patria est qui et post praeturam et consul maximis periculis rem publicam liberarat. Non in eo cui facta iniuria est sed in eis qui fecerunt sceleris et conscientiae poena permansit.*

Notum est Opimium in praetura Fregellas cepisse, quo facto visus est ceteros quoque nominis Latini socios male animatos repressisse, eundemque in consulatu Fulvium Flaccum consularem et C. Gracchum tribunicium oppressisse, ob quam invidiam postea iudicio circumventus est et in exsilium actus.

tribuni aerarii. Then on a second occasion a measure was put through by Pompey in his second consulship, the year of this speech *(55 B.C.)*, requiring that jurors should be chosen, contrary to previous practice, from the wealthiest in their respective groups in the centuries, but should be appointed for duty from the same three categories mentioned above.

(about 90 lines from the end)
[§95] *Expulsion from his country was the fate of L. Opimius, a man who after his praetorship and as consul had delivered the state from the most threatening dangers. But it was not the one who suffered injustice but those who inflicted it that were the victims of punishment - the punishment of the crime and their own awareness of guilt.*

It is a known fact that Opimius captured Fregellae during his praetorship *(125 B.C.)*; after that he seems to have crushed other allies with Latin status who proved rebellious; then during his consulship *(122 B.C.)* to have defeated the ex-consul Fulvius Flaccus and C. Gracchus the *tribunus plebis.* This brought him discredit, and he was later taken to court, convicted, and exiled.[13]

PRO SCAURO

[See N. H. Watts (Loeb trans.), E. S. Gruen, *The last generation of the Roman Republic*, pp. 331ff., E. Badian, *OCD²* s.v. Scaurus (2).]

Cicero's speech in defence of Scaurus was given at his trial in 54 on a charge of misconduct as governor of Sardinia (*res repetundae*) – a hazard regularly faced by a Roman politician returning from a province where he had served as governor. Besides the short passages quoted by Asconius, we possess two substantial extracts in the *Ambrosianus* and *Taurinensis* palimpsests. These texts, as well as Asconius' own comments, show us that the trial focused not so much on the facts of the case, but rather on the internal political stresses of Rome – another familiar feature.

In his *Exposition* Asconius draws attention to Scaurus' father, M. Aemilius Scaurus, who was consul in 115. The family was a *patricius* one, but its political and financial distinction had faltered for three generations, and the elder Scaurus had had to pursue his career in politics as though he were a *novus homo* (A. p. 37). Nevertheless, his marriage to a daughter of the Metellus family (who married the dictator Sulla after his death) is a mark of his success, and it is worth noting that his selection as *princeps senatus* was the work of the censors – one of them a Metellus. As Asconius points out (p. 33), it was on this reputation that the younger Scaurus was heavily dependent, although he too had married shrewdly – his wife Mucia was previously married to Pompey. For further details see *OCD²*, s.v. Scaurus 1, 2.

The main difficulty, then, in interpreting this Commentary concerns the figure of Pompey in the *Exposition* below, playing his ever-ambiguous game: his support for Scaurus was expected, since Scaurus had served under him as *quaestor* in about 65 (quite apart from their relationship by marriage just mentioned), and a man in that position could normally look to his *patronus* for assistance; yet that assistance was mysteriously not forthcoming. Indeed in 53, when Scaurus faced a charge of *ambitus* (bribery)

during his campaign for the consulship, Cicero's renewed eloquence was unavailing against Pompey's hostility, and Scaurus went into exile after his conviction.

II. PRO M. SCAVRO

(18) Hanc quoque orationem eisdem consulibus dixit quibus pro Vatinio, L. Domitio Ahenobarbo et Appio Claudio Pulchro coss.

Summus iudicii dies fuit a.d. IIII Nonas Septemb.

A R G V M E N T V M   H O C   E S T

M. Scaurus M. Scauri filius qui princeps senatus fuit vitricum habuit Sullam: quo victore et munifico in socios victoriae ita abstinens fuit ut nihil neque donari sibi voluerit neque ab hasta emerit. Aedilitatem summa magnificentia gessit, adeo ut in eius impensas opes suas absumpserit magnumque aes alienum contraxerit.

Ex praetura provinciam Sardiniam obtinuit, in qua neque satis abstinenter se gessisse existimatus est et valde arroganter: quod genus morum in eo paternum videbatur, cum cetera industria nequaquam esset par. Erat tamen aliquando inter patronos causarum et, postquam ex provincia redierat, dixerat pro C. Catone, isque erat absolutus a.d. IIII Nona Quint. Ipse cum ad consulatus petitionem a.d. III Kal. Quint. Romam redisset, querentibus de eo Sardis, a P. Valerio Triario, adulescente parato ad dicendum et notae industriae *(19)* – filio eius qui in Sardinia contra M. Lepidum arma tulerat et post in Asia legatus Pontoque L. Luculli fuerat, cum is bellum contra Mithridatem gereret – postulatus est apud M. Catonem praetorem repetundarum, ut in Actis scriptum est, pridie Nonas Quintil. post diem tertium quam C. Cato erat absolutus.

Subscripserunt Triario in Scaurum L. Marius L. f., M. et Q. Pacuvii fratres cognomine Claudi. Qui inquisitionis in Sardiniam itemque in Corsicam insulas dies tricenos acceperunt neque profecti sunt ad inquirendum: cuius rei hanc causam reddebant, quod interea comitia consularia futura essent; timere ergo se ne Scaurus ea pecunia quam a sociis abstulisset emeret consulatum et, sicut pater eius fecisset, ante quam de eo iudicari posset, magistratum iniret ac rursus ante alias provincias spoliaret quam

II. *Speech delivered on behalf of*
Marcus Aemilius Scaurus

(18) He delivered this speech in the same year as the one on behalf of Vatinius, when L. Domitius Ahenobarbus and Ap. Claudius Pulcher were consuls *(54 B.C.)*. The case ended on 2 September.

EXPOSITION

M. Scaurus was the son of the M. Scaurus who was leader of the senate; his stepfather was Sulla. When the latter after his victory was lavishly rewarding his supporters, Scaurus was such a model of restraint that he declined to receive any gifts, and made no purchases at the auctions. He made his term as *aedilis (58 B.C.)* a most glamorous affair, indeed in paying for it he used up his funds and fell into serious debt. After his praetorship *(56 B.C.)* he held the province of Sardinia, and was regarded as having behaved there with arrogance and insufficient restraint. In all this he seemed much like his father, though in energy he could not match him. He showed however some activity in the courts, and after returning from his province he spoke on behalf of C. Cato, who was acquitted on 4 July. Scaurus had returned to Rome on 29 June *(54 B.C.)* to stand for the consulship,[1] but the Sardinians laid a complaint about him, and he was prosecuted for *res repetundae* in front of M. Cato by P. Valerius Triarius, an eloquent and energetic young man *(19)* (this Triarius was the son of the man who had fought against M. Lepidus in Sardinia and who later on served under L. Lucullus in Asia and Pontus in the war against Mithridates) *(73–67 B.C.)*.

The prosecution took place, according to the *Acta*, on 6 July, the third day after C. Cato's acquittal. Triarius was supported by L. Marius son of Lucius and the brothers M. and Q. Pacuvius who carried the name Claudius. These men were each granted 30 days for their investigations in Sardinia and Corsica, but did not leave to begin their inquiries; they explained that the consular elections were imminent, and they were afraid that Scaurus might buy the consulship with the money he had extorted from the province, and then enter office before

rationem prioris administrationis redderet. Scaurus summam fiduciam in paterni nominis dignitate, magnam in necessitudine Cn. Pompeii Magni reponebat. Habebat enim filium liberorum Cn. Pompeii fratrem: nam Tertiam, Scaevolae filiam, dimissam a Pompeio in matrimonium duxerat. M. Catonem autem qui id iudicium, ut diximus, exercebat metuebat admodum propter amicitiam quae erat illi cum Triario: nam Flaminia, Triarii mater, et ipse Triarius sororem Catonis Serviliam, quae mater M. Bruti fuit, familiariter diligebat; ea porro apud Catonem maternam obtinebat auctoritatem. Sed in eo iudicio neque Pompeius propensum adiutorium praebuit - videbatur enim apud animum *(20)* eius non minus offensionis contraxisse, quod iudicium eius in Muciam crimine impudicitiae ab eo dimissam levius fecisse existimaretur, cum eam ipse probasset, quam gratiae adquisisse necessitudinis iure, quod ex eadem uterque liberos haberet - neque Cato ab aequitate ea quae et vitam eius et magistratum illum decebat quoquam deflexit. Post diem autem quartum quam postulatus erat Scaurus Faustus Sulla tum quaestor, filius Sullae Felicis, frater ex eadem matre Scauri servis eius vulneratis prosiluit ex lectica et questus est prope interemptum esse se a competitoribus Scauri et ambulare cum CCC armatis seque, si necesse esset, vim vi repulsurum.

Defenderunt Scaurum sex patroni, cum ad id tempus raro quisquam pluribus quam quattuor uteretur: at post bella civilia ante legem Iuliam ad duodenos patronos est perventum. Fuerunt autem hi sex: P. Clodius Pulcher, M. Marcellus, M. Calidius, M. Cicero, M. Messala Niger, Q. Hortensius. Ipse quoque Scaurus dixit pro se ac magnopere iudices movit et squalore et lacrimis et aedilitatis effusae memoria ac favore populari ac praecipue paternae auctoritatis recordatione.

E N A R R A T I O

CIRCA VER. A PRIM. XXXX

[I.1] Cum enumerat iudicia quae pater Scauri expertus est: *(21) Subiit etiam populi iudicium inquirente Cn. Domitio tribuno plebis.*

the case could come to court (like his father);[2] he might
then begin robbing other provinces before he could be
made to account for his earlier term of duty.

Scaurus relied heavily on his father's reputation and
on his own connection with Pompey: his son was the
brother of Pompey's children, since he had himself
married Pompey's ex-wife (Mucia) Tertia, daughter of
Scaevola. He was very nervous of M. Cato, who was to
preside over this case as I have said, the reason being
Cato's friendship with Triarius: Flaminia, the mother of
Triarius, and Triarius himself were very close to Cato's
sister Servilia, who was M. Brutus' mother; and in
addition she had an almost maternal influence over Cato.
However, Pompey did not in fact offer the expected
assistance, *(20)* since Scaurus seemed to have caused
offence to him by making Pompey's divorce of Mucia on
grounds of shameful conduct look insufficiently serious
(Scaurus had after all shown approval of her himself);
and this offence outweighed the influence Scaurus had
hoped for through the family relationship (both men
having had children by Mucia). On the other hand, Cato
did not abandon in the least the incorruptibility that
suited his way of life and his office. Four days after
Scaurus was charged, the quaestor Faustus Sulla, son of
Sulla Felix, who was Scaurus' half-brother, leapt from his
litter after an attack on his slaves and cried out that he
had been almost murdered by Scaurus' rivals – he was
therefore taking a bodyguard of 300 men and would meet
force with force if need be.

Scaurus was defended by six speakers (rarely
hitherto had anyone had more than four, though after the
Civil Wars until the Law of Iulius[3] the number reached
twelve). The six were: P. Clodius Pulcher, M. Marcellus, M.
Calidius, M. Cicero, M. Messala Niger, Q. Hortensius. In
addition Scaurus spoke on his own behalf, and greatly
impressed the jury by his unkempt clothing, his tears,
his references to his generosity as *aedilis*, his popularity,
and particularly his appeals to his father's reputation.

C O M M E N T A R Y

(about 40 lines from the start)
[I.1] Cicero lists the court cases in which Scaurus' father
was involved:
(21) He submitted to the judgment of the populus under

Cn. Domitius qui consul fuit cum C. Cassio, cum esset tribunus plebis, iratus Scauro quod eum in augurum collegium non cooptaverat, diem ei dixit apud populum et multam irrogavit, quod eius opera sacra populi Romani deminuta esse diceret. Crimini dabat sacra publica populi Romani deum Penatium quae Lavini fierent opera eius minus recte casteque fieri. Quo crimine absolutus est Scaurus quidem, sed ita ut a tribus tribubus damnaretur, a XXXII absolveretur, et in his pauca puncta inter damnationem et absolutionem interessent.

IBIDEM

[2] *Reus est factus a Q. Servilio Caepione lege Servilia, cum iudicia penes equestrem ordinem essent et P. Rutilio damnato nemo tam innocens videretur ut non timeret illa.*

Q. Servilius Caepio Scaurum ob legationis Asiaticae invidiam et adversus leges pecuniarum captarum reum fecit repetundarum lege quam tulit Servilius Glaucia.

Scaurus tanta fuit continentia animi et magnitudine ut Caepionem contra reum detulerit et breviore die inquisitionis accepta effecerit ut ille prior causam diceret; M. quoque Drusum tribunum plebis cohortatus sit ut iudicia commutaret.

(22) IBIDEM

[3] *Ab eodem etiam lege Varia custos ille rei publicae proditionis est in crimen vocatus: vexatus a Q. Vario tribuno plebis est.*

Non multo ante, Italico bello exorto, cum ob sociis negatam civitatem nobilitas in invidia esset, Q. Varius tr.pl. legem tulit ut quaereretur de iis quorum ope consiliove socii contra populum Romanum arma sumpsissent. Tum Q. Caepio vetus inimicus Scauri sperans se invenisse occasionem opprimendi eius egit ut Q. Varius tribunus plebis belli concitati crimine adesse apud se Scaurum iuberet anno LXXII. Ille per viatorem arcessitus, cum iam ex morbo male solveretur, dissuadentibus amicis

investigation by Cn. Domitius, tribunus plebis.

Cn. Domitius was consular colleague of C. Cassius (*96 B.C.*); while he was *tribunus plebis (104* or *103 B.C.)* he called Scaurus before the *populus,* out of resentment at not being appointed by him to the college of augurs, and demanded that he should be fined for inadequate performance of the sacred rituals. According to him the rituals of the Penates at Lavinium were not being properly and duly conducted. Scaurus was indeed acquitted, but three tribes supported conviction, while 32 went for acquittal, though even so by a narrow margin.

(in the same passage)
[I.2] *He was charged by Q. Servilius Caepio under the Servilian Law, at a time when the* equites *controlled the juries; and since P. Rutilius' conviction even the innocent went in fear of them.*

Q. Servilius Caepio charged Scaurus with *res repetundae* under the law of Servilius Glaucia *(tr.pl. 104 and 101 B.C.),* because of the hostility aroused by Scaurus' mission to Asia towards the laws concerned with stolen wealth. Scaurus possessed such coolness and nerve that he in turn charged Caepio, was given a shorter period for his inquiries, and induced him to plead his defence first; he further urged M. Drusus, *tribunus plebis,* to alter the composition of the juries.

(22) (in the same passage)
[I.3] *This guardian of the state was even charged under the law of Varius by the same men with betrayal; indeed he was harried by the* tribunus plebis *Q. Varius himself.*

A short while previously the Italian War had broken out, and Rome's *nobiles* were widely criticized for refusing to grant citizenship to her allies; so Q. Varius, a *tribunus plebis (90 B.C.),* promoted a law to set up an investigation into those who had given assistance or advice to the allies in their declaration of war against the Roman *populus.* Then Q. Caepio, being an old adversary of Scaurus, and thinking that he had uncovered an opportunity to destroy him, arranged for Q. Varius, *tribunus plebis,* to summon Scaurus to appear before him, at the age of 72, on a charge of promoting the war. When summoned by the bailiff, Scaurus was recovering with difficulty from an illness, and his friends urged him not to expose himself to public hostility at his age and state

ne se in illa valetudine et aetate invidiae populi obiceret, innixus nobilissimis iuvenibus processit in forum, deinde accepto respondendi loco dixit:

"Q. Varius Hispanus M. Scaurum principem senatus socios in arma ait convocasse; M. Scaurus princeps senatus negat; testis nemo est: utri vos, Quirites, convenit credere?"

Qua voce ita omnium commutavit animos ut ab ipso etiam tribuno dimitteretur.

Dicit iterum de patre M. Scauri:
[4] *Non enim tantum admiratus sum ego illum virum, sicut omnes, sed etiam praecipue dilexi. Primus enim me flagrantem studio laudis in spem impulit posse virtute me sine praesidio fortunae quo contendissem labore et constantia pervenire.*

(23) Possit aliquis quaerere cur hoc dixerit Cicero, cum Scaurus patricius fuerit: quae generis claritas etiam inertes homines ad summos honores provexit. Verum Scaurus ita fuit patricius ut tribus supra eum aetatibus iacuerit domus eius fortuna. Nam neque pater neque avus neque etiam proavus – ut puto, propter tenues opes et nullam vitae industriam – honores adepti sunt. Itaque Scauro aeque ac novo homini laborandum fuit.

[5] *Si, me hercule, iudices, pro L. Tubulo dicerem quem unum ex omni memoria sceleratissimum et audacissimum fuisse accepimus, tamen non timerem, venenum hospiti aut convivae si diceretur cenanti ab illo datum cui neque heres neque iratus fuisset.*

L. hic Tubulus praetorius fuit aetate patrum Ciceronis. Is propter multa flagitia cum de exsilio arcessitus esset ut in carcere necaretur, venenum bibit.

CIRCA TERTIAM PARTEM A PRIMO

[II.1] *Illa audivimus; hoc vero meminimus ac paene vidimus, eiusdem stirpis et nominis P. Crassum, ne in manus incideret inimicorum, se ipsum interemisse.*

Hic Crassus fuit pater Crassi eius qui aemulus potentiae Cn. Pompeii fuit. Periit autem in dominatione L.

of health; nevertheless he came to the forum, leaning on certain young *nobiles*, and when given the chance to reply he said: "Q. Varius Hispanus asserts that M. Scaurus, the leader of the senate, called upon the allies to resort to war; M. Scaurus, leader of the senate, denies the accusation: there is no witness; Quirites, which of us do you choose to believe?" With these words he transformed everyone's attitude, and the *tribunus plebis* himself let him go.

He says further about Scaurus' father:
[I.4] *I have not merely admired him, as everyone has: I have felt for him an especial affection. When I was consumed with a desire for fame, he managed to convince me that without the help of good luck I could deservedly reach my objective by determination and hard work.*
(23) You may wonder why Cicero says this, Scaurus being a *patricius*; after all the distinction of this class of men has brought even the incompetent to the highest eminence. The reason is that though he was a *patricius* the fortunes of his family had been at a low ebb for three generations: father, grandfather, and great-grandfather had all failed to achieve eminence, presumably because they had slender resources and little energy. So Scaurus had to put in effort just like a *novus homo*.

[I.5] *L. Tubulus, gentlemen, is certainly the most unscrupulous and reckless person that history records: now supposing I were speaking on his behalf, I should not feel the least alarm if it were alleged that he had given poison to a visitor or dinner-guest, provided he was not hostile to him, nor stood to inherit from him.*
L. Tubulus was a man of praetorian rank in the generation previous to Cicero; because of his record of crime, he was called back from exile to face death in prison, but took poison first.

(about a third of the way through the speech)
[II.1] *That is hearsay; but we remember the occasion, and were virtually witnesses, when P. Crassus, a man of the same family, took his own life rather than fall into his enemies' hands.*
This Crassus was the father of the Crassus who was

Cinnae, cum ille et alios principes optimatum et collegam suum Cn. Octavium occidit.

(24) [STATIM

[2] *Ac neque illius Crassi factum superioris isdem honoribus usus, qui fortissimus in bellis fuisset, M'. Aquilius potuit imitari.*

Haec verba quibus Cicero nunc utitur, *ac neque*, eam videntur habere naturam ut semel poni non soleant; quia est coniunctio disiunctiva et semper postulat ut rursus inferatur *neque*, ut cum dicimus *neque hoc neque illud.* Quo autem casu acciderit quave ratione ut hoc loco Cicero hoc verbo ita usus sit, praesertim cum adiecerit illam appositionem, ut non intulerit postea alterum, *neque* perspicere potui et attendendum esse valde puto: moveor enim merita viri auctoritate. Neque ignoro aliquando hoc verbum *neque* vel semel poni, ut in eadem hac oratione ante ipse Cicero posuit: *Sic, inquam, se, iudices, res habet; neque hoc a me novum disputatur sed quaesitum ab aliis est.* Sed hoc loco et sine praepositione illius verbi videmus esse positum, et tamen quasi secundum aliquid inferri. Nam cum dixerit *neque hoc a me novum disputatur*, infert *sed quaesitum ab aliis est.*]

PAVLO POST

[2] *Quid vero alterum Crassum temporibus isdem – num aut clarissimi viri Iulii aut summo ingenio praeditus M. Antonius potuit imitari?*

(25) Hic alter Crassus idem est de quo supra diximus. Alterum autem eum appellat, quia ante mentionem fecit P. Crassi qui fuit pontifex maximus et bello Aristonici in Asia dedit operam ut occideretur. Iulios autem cum dicit, duos Caesares fratres C. et L. significat: ex quibus Lucius et consul et censor fuit, Gaius aedilicius quidem occisus est, sed tantum in civitate potuit ut causa belli civilis contentio eius cum Sulpicio tr. fuerit. Nam et sperabat et id agebat Caesar ut omissa praetura consul fieret: cui cum primis temporibus iure Sulpicius resisteret, postea nimia contentione ad ferrum et ad arma processit. Idem inter primos temporis sui oratores et tragicus poeta bonus admodum habitus est; huius sunt enim tragoediae quae

Pompey's great rival. He died under the régime of L. Cinna *(87–84 B.C.)*, who put to death his own colleague Cn. Octavius and other *optimates.*

(24) [(immediately after this passage)
[II.2] *And nor could that deed of the elder Crassus be matched by M'. Aquilius, a man who had been courageous in war and had reached the same eminence.*

The words that Cicero uses here – "and nor" – are like one another in not normally being used singly; "nor" is a disjunctive conjunction that always requires a counterpart: we say "nor this nor that". How Cicero came to do what he did here, in using the word singly, "nor" can I understand "and" think deserves consideration; for the orator's justified authority impresses me. I am aware that the word "nor" is used singly, as for instance earlier in this same speech: *Such, gentlemen, is the state of affairs; nor is this a fresh question that I ask, but one asked by others also.* But here we see it placed at the start of the sentence and appearing to anticipate a second point. For when he says "nor is this a fresh question that I ask", the word leads us to "but one asked by others also".]⁴

(shortly afterwards)
[II.2] *As for the younger Crassus at this same time – could the distinguished Julian family or the acute intellect of M. Antonius equal him?*
(25) This "younger" Crassus is the one mentioned earlier, called "younger" because Cicero has already spoken of the P. Crassus who was chief priest and saw to it that Aristonicus met his death in the war in Asia. The "Julians" are the two brothers C. and L. Caesar: Lucius was consul *(90 B.C.)* and *censor (89 B.C.)*, while Gaius was killed having reached only the position of *aedilis (90 B.C.)*; but the latter had such influence in public life that his struggle with the *tribunus plebis* Sulpicius was a cause of civil war. Caesar intended to be consul without having first been praetor, and was trying to bring this about; at first Sulpicius rightly obstructed him, but later pressed his obstruction overmuch and resorted to violence. This Caesar was thought to be one of the foremost orators of his time and a most impressive writer of tragedies; some of these exist, labelled with his authorship. These two Caesars and Antonius were killed

inscribuntur Iuli. Et hi autem Iulii et Antonius a satellitibus Mari sunt occisi, cum Crassus, ut supra diximus, eundem casum sua manu praevenisset.

CIR. MEDIVM

[33sq.] *Neque vero haec ipsa cotidiana res Appium Claudium illa humanitate et sapientia praeditum per se ipsa movisset, nisi hunc C. Claudi fratris sui competitorem fore putasset. Qui sive patricius sive plebeius esset – nondum enim certum constitutum erat – cum illo sibi contentionem fore putabat.*

Fuerunt enim duae familiae Claudiae: earum quae Marcellorum *(26)* appellata est plebeia, quae Pulchrorum patricia. Sed hoc loco urbane Cicero lusit in C. Claudium, cum quo in gratiam non redierat. Nam quia is P. Clodi erat frater qui ex patricia in plebeiam familiam transierat per summam infamiam, eum quoque dubitare adhuc dixit.

POST DVAS PARTES ORATIONIS

Dicit dein de Scauro quem defendit:
[45] *Nam cum ex multis unus ei restaret Dolabella paternus inimicus qui cum Q. Caepione propinquo suo contra Scaurum patrem suum subsignaverat: eas sibi inimicitias non susceptas sed relictas et cetera.*

Ne forte erretis et eundem hunc Cn. Dolabellam putetis esse in quem C. Caesaris orationes legitis, scire vos oportet duos eodem eo tempore fuisse et praenomine et nomine et cognomine Dolabellas. Horum igitur alterum Caesar accusavit nec damnavit; alterum M. Scaurus et accusavit et damnavit.

POST TRES PARTES A PRIMO

Quo loco defendit, quod tam magnificam domum Scaurus habet:
[45] *Praesertim cum propinquitas et celebritas loci suspicionem desidiae tollat aut cupiditatis.*

(27) Demonstrasse vobis memini me hanc domum in ea parte Palatii esse quae, cum ab Sacra via descenderis et per proximum vicum qui est a sinistra parte prodieris, posita est. Possidet eam nunc Largus Caecina qui consul fuit cum Claudio. In huius domus atrio fuerunt quattuor columnae marmoreae insigni magnitudine quae nunc esse

by agents of Marius, while Crassùs, as I have said,
preempted this fate by suicide.

(about half way)
[II.33ff.] *Now Appius Claudius being a civilized and
intelligent man, this unremarkable fact would not have
disturbed him on its own, had it not been his suspicion
that this man would be a rival of his brother C. Claudius.
And whether this brother was to be* patricius *or* plebeius
*- a question undecided as yet - he thought he would face
conflict with my client.*

There were two Claudius families, *(26)* the one
plebeius and surnamed Marcellus and one *patricius*,
surnamed Pulcher. However, at this point Cicero makes a
witty joke about C. Claudius, since at the time he was not
on good terms with him: Claudius was the brother of the
P. Clodius who had been transferred from the *patricius* to
the *plebeius* branch amid great scandal *(59 B.C.)*, and
Cicero pretends that Claudius himself is still hesitating
about whether to do the same.

(two thirds of the way through the speech)
Now Cicero speaks of his client Scaurus:
[II.45] *Of the many opponents of his father there remained Dolabella alone, who had joined the attack with his
relative Q. Caepio; these hostilities being not devised by
him but inherited, etc.*

Do not make the mistake of thinking that this is the
Cn. Dolabella who was the victim of C. Caesar's speeches;
there were at the time two Dolabellas with all three names
identical. One was prosecuted unsuccessfully by Caesar,[5]
the other successfully by M. Scaurus.

(three quarters of the way through)
Here he defends Scaurus' possession of a magnificent
house:
[II.45] *In particular the fact that the place is near at
hand and lively prevents one suspecting idleness or
avarice.*
(27) I remember mentioning that this house is in the
Palatine district, the first turning on the left as you come
down the Sacred Way; it is now the property of Caecina
Largus, the consular colleague *(A.D. 42)* of Claudius. In
the hall of this house there used to be four massive
marble columns which are now said to be in the colonnade

in regia theatri Marcelli dicuntur. Vsus erat iis aedilis -
ut ipse quoque significat - in ornatu theatri quod ad
tempus perquam amplae magnitudinis fecerat.

VER. A NOV. ***

[45] *Haec cum tu effugere non potuisses, contendes tamen
et postulabis ut M. Aemilius cum sua dignitate omni, cum
patris memoria, cum avi gloria, sordidissimae, vanissimae,
levissimae genti ac prope dicam pellitis testibus
condonetur?*

Avum hunc Scauri maternum significat L. Metellum
pontificem maximum, quem postea nominat quoque. Nam
paternus avus proavusque Scauri humiles atque obscuri
fuerunt.

VER. A NOVIS. CLX

[46] *Vndique mihi suppeditat quod pro M. Scauro dicam,
quocumque non modo mens verum etiam oculi inciderunt.
Curia illa vos de gravissimo (28) principatu patris
fortissimoque testatur; L. ipse Metellus, avus huius,
sanctissimos deos illo constituisse templo videtur in vestro
conspectu, iudices, ut salutem a vobis nepotis sui
deprecarentur.*

Castoris et Pollucis templum Metellus quem nominat
refecerat.

Laudaverunt Scaurum consulares novem, L. Piso, L.
Volcacius, Q. Metellus Nepos, M. Perpenna, L. Philippus, M.
Cicero, Q. Hortensius, P. Servilius Isauricus pater, Cn.
Pompeius Magnus. Horum magna pars per tabellas laudaverunt quia aberant: inter quos Pompeius quoque; nam
quod erat pro cos. extra urbem morabatur. Vnus praeterea
adulescens laudavit, frater eius, Faustus Cornelius Sullae
filius. Is in laudatione multa humiliter et cum lacrimis
locutus non minus audientes permovit quam Scaurus ipse
permoverat. Ad genua iudicum, cum sententiae ferrentur,
bifariam se diviserunt qui pro eo rogabant: ab uno latere
Scaurus ipse et M'. Glabrio, sororis filius, et L. Paulus et
P. Lentulus, Lentuli Nigri flaminis filius, et L. Aemilius
Buca filius et C. Memmius, Fausta natus, supplicaverunt;
ex altera parte Sulla Faustus, frater Scauri, et T. Annius
Milo, cui Fausta ante paucos menses nupserat dimissa a
Memmio, et C. Peducaeus et C. Cato et M. Laenas

of Marcellus' theatre. When he was *aedilis* he used them, as we know from him, to decorate the enormous theatre which he built then.

([. . .] lines from the end)
[II.45] *Being unable to evade this argument, will you then insist and demand that M. Aemilius, his eminence, the repute of his father, the fame of his grandfather, that all these should be surrendered to a squalid, contemptible, and worthless band of (you might almost say) goatskin-clad witnesses?*

He means Scaurus' maternal grandfather, the chief priest L. Metellus, whom he names later on. Scaurus' paternal grandfather and great-grandfather were men of humble and obscure origin.

(160 lines from the end)
[II.46] *Wherever my mind and my gaze falls, I find support for my defence of M. Scaurus. The senate-chamber bears witness (28) to the profound and courageous leadership of his father; and it seems that his grandfather L. Metellus installed the holy gods in that temple within your view so that they could require of you the preservation of his grandson.*

The temple mentioned is that of Castor and Pollux, rebuilt by Metellus.

Scaurus was commended by nine ex-consuls: L. Piso, L. Volcacius, Q. Metellus Nepos, M. Perpenna, L. Philippus, M. Cicero, Q. Hortensius, P. Servilius Isauricus senior, and Pompey. Most of these sent written commendations, as they were away from Rome, including Pompey who as pro-consul was waiting outside the city. In addition one young man, the brother of Scaurus - Faustus Cornelius son of Sulla - gave his support. In his speech he spoke at length, humbly and tearfully, and touched the listeners just as much as Scaurus himself. When the vote was being taken, Scaurus' supporters divided into two groups at the jurymen's knees: on one side Scaurus, M'. Glabrio his sister's son, L. Paulus, P. Lentulus brother of Lentulus Niger the priest, L. Aemilius Buca his son, and C. Memmius son of Fausta, all knelt in prayer; on the other side Faustus Sulla brother of Scaurus, T. Annius Milo who was married a few months previously to Fausta the divorced wife of Memmius, C. Peducaeus, C. Cato, M.

Curtianus.

Sententias tulerunt senatores duo et XX, equites tres et XX, tribuni aerarii XXV: ex quibus damnaverunt senatores IIII, equites II, tribuni II.

(29) Cato praetor, Cicero cum vellet de accusatoribus in consilium mittere multique e populo manus in accusatores intenderent, cessit imperitae multitudini ac postero die in consilium de calumnia accusatorum misit. P. Triarius nullam gravem sententiam habuit; subscriptores eius M. et Q. Pacuvii fratres denas et L. Marius tres graves habuerunt.

Cato praetor iudicium, quia aestate agebatur, sine tunica exercuit campestri sub toga cinctus. In forum quoque sic descendebat iusque dicebat, idque repetierat ex vetere consuetudine secundum quam et Romuli et Tati statuae in Capitolio et in rostris Camilli fuerunt togatae sine tunicis.

Laenas Curtianus. There were 22 senators' votes, 23 from the *equites*, 25 from the *tribuni aerarii*; votes in favour of conviction were: senators 4, *equites* 2, *tribuni aerarii* 2.

(29) Cicero then wished to report the prosecutors to a committee, and a large crowd began threatening them; so the praetor Cato gave in to this unsophisticated gathering, and the next day put to a committee the possibility of the prosecution having been vexatious. P. Triarius was the victim of no serious complaint, while the brothers M. and Q. Pacuvius sustained ten each and L. Marius three.

Since the case was heard during the summer, the praetor Cato conducted it wearing a loin-cloth under his toga and no tunic. He came to the forum and announced the verdict in the same clothing, there being (he asserted) an ancient tradition reflected in the fact that the statues of Romulus and Tatius on the Capitol and the platform of Camillus show them wearing a toga and no tunic.

PRO MILONE

[See N. H. Watts (Loeb trans. - includes translation of *Exposition*); A. C. Clark, commentary in his edition of *pro Milone* (Oxford 1895); M. Grant, *Cicero: Selected Political Speeches* (Penguin); E. S. Gruen, *The last generation of the Roman Republic*, pp. 337ff.]

The decade of the 50s, especially from 55 onwards, was a period of growing violence and disorder. For some time there had been an increasing extremism in the practice of politics: the First Triumvirate had acquiesced in the removal of Cicero from Rome by P. Clodius Pulcher (see above, Introduction to *In Pisonem*, A. p. 1); and it was Clodius who as *tribunus plebis* in 58 introduced a bill to legalize the existence of *collegia* (originally these had been guilds of craftsmen, but they had great potential value when organized into electoral pressure groups and, in due course, into instruments for promoting violence as a political weapon). Amidst these developments the figures of Clodius and T. Annius Milo seem to stand out as somewhat characteristic - alike in their methods, though supported by politicians of opposing interests. In the lengthy account of the affray at Bovillae given by Asconius the question is prominent: which of the two provoked the other? They had both, in 53, been competing for political office, Milo for the consulship and Clodius for the praetorship, while the elections themselves were repeatedly postponed (see *Exposition* below, A. p. 51). When Milo's trial for murder came up in the next year, Cicero responded to the obligation to defend his ally; but over the event hovered the figure of Pompey, ambiguous as ever; he had now been declared consul with no colleague, on the recommendation of M. Bibulus and M. Cato in default of elections. Of his fellow Triumvirs, Caesar was fully occupied in Gaul, while M. Crassus had departed two years previously to seek military glory against Parthia as governor of the frontier province of Syria; and there he had perished at the battle of Carrhae in 53.

The trial of Milo opened with Pompey's troops surrounding the court, and Cicero's actual defence

was apparently rather less eloquent than the published version we possess (A. p. 65). He failed to gain his client's acquittal, and Milo began his exile in Marseille with a copy of the revised speech as bedtime reading.

III. PRO MILONE

(30) Orationem hanc dixit Cn. Pompeio III cos. a.d. VII
Id. April. Quod iudicium cum ageretur, exercitum in foro
et in omnibus templis quae circum forum sunt collocatum a
Cn. Pompeio fuisse non tantum ex oratione et annalibus,
sed etiam ex libro apparet qui Ciceronis nomine inscribitur de optimo genere oratorum.

A R G V M E N T V M   H O C   E S T

T. Annius Milo et P. Plautius Hypsaeus et Q. Metellus
Scipio consulatum petierunt non solum largitione palam
profusa sed etiam factionibus armatorum succincti.

Miloni et Clodio summae erant inimicitiae, quod et Milo
Ciceronis erat amicissimus in reducendoque eo enixe
operam tr.pl. dederat, et P. Clodius restituto quoque
Ciceroni erat infestissimus ideoque summe studebat
Hypsaeo et Scipioni contra Milonem.

Ac saepe inter se Milo et Clodius cum suis factionibus
Romae depugnaverant: et erant uterque audacia pares, sed
Milo pro melioribus partibus stabat. Praeterea in eundem
annum consulatum Milo, Clodius praeturam petebat, quam
debilem futuram consule Milone intellegebat.

Deinde cum diu tracta essent comitia consularia
perficique ob eas ipsas perditas candidatorum *(31)*
contentiones non possent, et ob id mense Ianuario nulli
dum neque consules neque praetores essent trahereturque
dies eodem quo antea modo - cum Milo quam primum comitia confici vellet confideretque cum bonorum studiis, quod
obsistebat Clodio, tum etiam populo propter effusas
largitiones impensasque ludorum scaenicorum ac gladiatorii
muneris maximas, in quas tria patrimonia effudisse eum
Cicero significat; competitores eius trahere vellent,
ideoque Pompeius gener Scipionis et T. Munatius tribunus
plebis referri ad senatum de patriciis convocandis qui
interregem proderent non essent passi, cum interregem
prodere stata res esset -: a.d. XIII Kal. Febr. - Acta

III. *Speech delivered on behalf of Milo*

(30) Cicero gave this speech on 7 April in the third consulship of Pompey *(52 B.C.)*. During the trial Pompey stationed troops in the forum and the temples sur-rounding it, a fact evident not only from the speech and the standard histories, but also from the book in Cicero's name entitled *The Ideal Orator*.

EXPOSITION

T. Annius Milo, P. Plautius Hypsaeus, and Q. Metellus Scipio were rival candidates for the consulship; largesse was openly distributed, and they furthermore surrounded themselves with squads of armed men. A fierce feud existed between Milo and Clodius, since Milo was a firm friend of Cicero and had given strenuous support as *tribunus plebis* to Cicero's recall from exile *(57 B.C.)*; after Cicero's return P. Clodius remained just as hostile towards Cicero, and so backed Hypsaeus and Scipio against Milo. Frequently Milo and Clodius fought out their feud in Rome with their own gangs: they were both equally ruthless, but Milo acted for the *meliores*. Now while Milo was standing for the consulship Clodius was campaigning, in the same year, for the praetorship; and he reckoned that his tenure would be undermined if Milo achieved the position of consul. The consular elections were considerably delayed, and it became impossible to complete them because of the reckless hostilities of the candidates; *(31)* hence by January there were still no consuls or praetors in office, and election-day was all the time being postponed as before. Milo in fact wanted the elections to be completed as soon as might be: he felt confident of the support of the *boni* (since he was opposing Clodius) and of the *populus*, since he had been generous in his largesse and had paid for sumptuous theatrical performances and gladiatorial shows (at a cost of three personal fortunes, according to Cicero).[1] The other candidates preferred delay, and so the *tribunus plebis* T. Munatius and Pompey (son-in-law of Scipio) had objected to a proposal being put to the senate for an assembly of *patricii* to install an *interrex* – that being the traditional procedure in such a situation.

etenim magis sequenda et ipsam orationem, quae Actis congruit, puto quam Fenestellam qui a.d. XIIII Kal. Febr. tradit – Milo Lanuvium, ex quo erat municipio et ubi tum dictator, profectus est ad flaminem prodendum postera die.

Occurrit ei circa horam nonam Clodius paulo ultra Bovillas, rediens ab Aricia, prope eum locum in quo Bonae Deae sacellum est; erat autem allocutus decuriones Aricinorum. Vehebatur Clodius equo; servi XXX fere expediti, ut illo tempore mos erat iter facientibus, gladiis cincti sequebantur. Erant cum Clodio praeterea tres comites eius, ex quibus eques Romanus unus C. Causinius Schola, duo de plebe noti homines P. Pomponius, C. Clodius. Milo raeda vehebatur cum uxore Fausta, filia L. Sullae dictatoris, et M. Fufio familiari suo. Sequebatur eos *(32)* magnum servorum agmen, inter quos gladiatores quoque erant, ex quibus duo noti Eudamus et Birria. Ii in ultimo agmine tardius euntes cum servis P. Clodi rixam commiserunt. Ad quem tumultum cum respexisset Clodius minitabundus, umerum eius Birria rumpia traiecit. Inde cum orta esset pugna, plures Miloniani accurrerunt. Clodius vulneratus in tabernam proximam in Bovillano delatus est.

Milo ut cognovit vulneratum Clodium, cum sibi periculosius illud etiam vivo eo futurum intellegeret, occiso autem magnum solacium esset habiturus, etiam si subeunda esset poena, exturbari taberna iussit. Fuit antesignanus servorum eius M. Saufeius. Atque ita Clodius latens extractus est multisque vulneribus confectus. Cadaver eius in via relictum, quia servi Clodi aut occisi erant aut graviter saucii latebant, Sex. Taedius senator, qui forte ex rure in urbem revertebatur, sustulit et lectica sua Romam ferri iussit; ipse rursus eodem unde erat egressus se recepit.

Perlatum est corpus Clodi ante primam noctis horam, infimaeque plebis et servorum maxima multitudo magno luctu corpus in atrio domus positum circumstetit. Augebat autem facti invidiam uxor Clodi Fulvia quae cum effusa lamentatione vulnera eius ostendebat. Maior postera die luce prima multitudo eiusdem generis confluxit, compluresque noti homines visi sunt. Erat domus Clodi ante paucos menses empta de M. Scauro in Palatio: eodem

Now on 20 January (I regard it as desirable to follow
the evidence of the *Acta* and this very speech - which
are in agreement - rather than Fenestella who reports 19
January) Milo set out for Lanuvium, his home town of
which he was then *dictator*, to install a priest the next
day. At about 3 p.m. just beyond Bovillae he was
confronted by Clodius, who was on his way back from
Aricia where he had been addressing the town officials;
the spot was quite near the shrine of Bona Dea. Clodius
was on horseback, with about 30 slaves armed with
swords and unencumbered, the usual practice when on
the move in those days. In addition he had three friends
with him, one an *eques* called C. Causinius Schola and two
who were well-known *plebeii*: P. Pomponius and C. Clodius.
Milo was travelling in a carriage with his wife Fausta,
daughter of the *dictator* L. Sulla, and a relative called M.
Fufius; *(32)* behind them was a long column of slaves
including some gladiators, such as the famous Eudamus
and Birria. They were at the far end of the line, moving
fairly slowly, and they started a brawl with Clodius'
slaves. As Clodius glanced back menacingly at this
uproar, Birria hurled a lance which pierced his shoulder.
With the fight under way, more of Milo's entourage ran
up, while the wounded Clodius was carried to a near-by
inn in Bovillae.

Milo heard that he had been injured, and decided
that it would be dangerous to leave Clodius alive, while
his death would be a relief, even if there were penalties
to be paid; so he had Clodius turned out of the inn. The
superintendent of Milo's slaves was called M. Saufeius.
The desperately wounded Clodius then was hauled out
unobserved, and his body was left in the road: Clodius'
slaves were either dead or lying low with grave injuries.
It was picked up by a senator Sex. Teidius, who
happened to be returning to Rome from the country; he
had the body taken to Rome in his litter, and retraced
his steps the way he had come. The corpse reached Rome
before about 7 p.m., and was surrounded in the hall of
Clodius' house by a great crowd of slaves and rabble,
weeping copiously; and the feeling aroused by the affair
was intensified by his wife Fulvia,[2] who displayed his
wounds with unrestrained grief. At dawn the next day a
still bigger crowd of the same sort gathered, and several
well-known men were seen there. Clodius' house, which he
had bought from M. Scaurus a few months earlier, was on

T. Munatius Plancus, frater L. Planci oratoris, et Q. Pompeius Rufus, Sullae dictatoris ex filia nepos, tribuni *(33)* plebis accurrerunt: eisque hortantibus vulgus imperitum corpus nudum ac calcatum, sicut in lecto erat positum, ut vulnera videri possent in forum detulit et in rostris posuit.

Ibi pro contione Plancus et Pompeius qui competitoribus Milonis studebant invidiam Miloni fecerunt. Populus duce Sex. Clodio scriba corpus P. Clodi in curiam intulit cremavitque subselliis et tribunalibus et mensis et codicibus librariorum; quo igne et ipsa quoque curia flagravit, et item Porcia basilica quae erat ei iuncta ambusta est.

Domus quoque M. Lepidi interregis – is enim magistratus curulis erat creatus – et absentis Milonis eadem illa Clodiana multitudo oppugnavit, sed inde sagittis repulsa est. Tum fasces ex luco Libitinae raptos attulit ad domum Scipionis et Hypsaei, deinde ad hortos Cn. Pompeii, clamitans eum modo consulem, modo dictatorem.

Incendium curiae maiorem aliquanto indignationem civitatis moverat quam interfectio Clodi. Itaque Milo, quem opinio fuerat ivisse in voluntarium exsilium, invidia adversariorum recreatus nocte ea redierat Romam qua incensa erat curia. Petebatque nihil deterritus consulatum; aperte quoque tributim in singulos milia assium dederat. Contionem ei post aliquot dies dedit M. Caelius tribunus plebis ac Cicero ipse etiam causam egit ad populum. Dicebant uterque Miloni a Clodio factas esse insidias.

Fiebant interea alii ex aliis interreges, quia comitia consularia *(34)* propter eosdem candidatorum tumultus et easdem manus armatas haberi non poterant.

Itaque primo factum erat S.C. ut interrex et tribuni plebis et Cn. Pompeius, qui pro cos. ad urbem erat, viderent ne quid detrimenti res publica caperet, dilectus autem Pompeius tota Italia haberet. Qui cum summa celeritate praesidium comparasset, postulaverunt apud eum familiam Milonis, item Faustae uxoris eius exhibendam duo adulescentuli qui Appii Claudii ambo appellabantur; qui filii erant C. Claudi, qui frater fuerat Clodi, et ob id illi patrui sui mortem velut auctore patre persequebantur.

the Palatine; here assembled T. Munatius Plancus the
brother of the orator L. Plancus, and Q. Pompeius Rufus
grandson of the *dictator* Sulla through his daughter –
both *tribuni plebis*. *(33)* At their suggestion the ignorant
mob carried the body to the forum, naked and battered
as it was, in the same attitude as it had had on its
couch, so that the wounds were clearly visible; then they
placed it on the speaker's platform. Plancus and Pompeius, being supporters of Milo's rivals, held a *contio*
there and inflamed people against Milo. Then the clerk
Sex. Cloelius persuaded the *populus* to take the body into
the senate-house and cremate it, using benches, tables,
other furniture, and notebooks belonging to the clerks;
this set fire to the senate-house itself, and the blaze
spread to the Basilica Porcia next door. Furthermore, the
Clodius crowd attacked the homes of Milo (who was away)
and of the *interrex* M. Lepidus (who had eventually been
appointed to this office), but they were driven back with
arrows. Then they grabbed the axes from the grove of
Libitina and brought them to Scipio's house and to
Hypsaeus', then to Pompey's garden villa, calling upon
him variously as consul and as *dictator*.

The destruction of the senate-house caused a good
deal more feeling among the public than the death of
Clodius. It was assumed that Milo had gone into voluntary
exile, but he was reassured by his opponents' unpopularity and returned to Rome on the night of the fire.
Then he resumed undaunted his campaign for the consulship; indeed he had openly presented each voter in the
tribes with 1000 *asses*. A few days later *contiones* were
held by a *tribunus plebis* M. Caelius and Cicero himself
before the *populus*, both men asserting that Milo had
been ambushed by Clodius.

Meanwhile a succession of *interreges* held office, *(34)*
since consular elections still could not be conducted
owing to the disorderliness of the candidates and the
activities of gangs. Then a senatorial decree was enacted
as a first step, requiring that the *interrex*, the *tribuni
plebis*, and Pompey, who remained as proconsul outside
the city, should "ensure that the state should suffer no
harm", and that Pompey should levy troops throughout
Italy. He very quickly organized a force, and then two
young men both called Appius Claudius lodged with him a
summons to appear, naming the *familia* of Milo and of his
wife Fausta. (These two men were sons of Clodius'

Easdem Faustae et Milonis familias postulaverunt duo Valerii, Nepos et Leo. L. Herennius Balbus P. Clodi quoque familiam et comitum eius postulavit; eodem tempore Caelius familiam Hypsaei et Q. Pompeii postulavit.

Adfuerunt Miloni Q. Hortensius, M. Cicero, M. Marcellus, M. Calidius, M. Cato, Faustus Sulla. Verba pauca Q. Hortensius dixit, liberos esse eos qui pro servis postularentur; nam post recentem caedem manu miserat eos Milo sub hoc titulo quod caput suum ulti essent. Haec agebantur mense intercalari.

Post diem tricesimum fere quam erat Clodius occisus Q. Metellus Scipio in senatu contra Q. Caepionem conquestus est de hac caede P. Clodi.

Falsum esse dixit, quod Milo sic se defenderet, sed Clodium Aricinos decuriones alloquendi gratia abisse profectum cum sex ac XX servis; Milonem subito post horam *(35)* quartam, senatu misso, cum servis amplius CCC armatis obviam ei contendisse et supra Bovillas inopinantem in itinere aggressum. Ibi P. Clodium tribus vulneribus acceptis Bovillas perlatum; tabernam in quam perfugerat expugnatam a Milone; semianimem Clodium extractum ... in via Appia occisum esse anulumque eius ei morienti extractum. Deinde Milonem, cum sciret in Albano parvolum filium Clodi esse, venisse ad villam et, cum puer ante subtractus esset, ex servo Halicore quaestionem ita habuisse ut eum articulatim consecaret; vilicum et duos praeterea servos iugulasse. Ex servis Clodi qui dominum defenderant undecim esse interfectos, Milonis duos solos saucios factos esse: ob quae Milonem postero die XII servos qui maxime operam navassent manu misisse populoque tributim singula milia aeris ad defendendos de se rumores dedisse. Milo misisse ad Cn. Pompeium dicebatur qui Hypsaeo summe studebat, quod fuerat eius quaestor, desistere se petitione consulatus, si ita ei videretur; Pompeius respondisse nemini se neque petendi neque desistendi auctorem esse, neque populi Romani potestatem aut consilio aut sententia interpellaturum. Deinde per C. Lucilium, qui propter M. Ciceronis familiaritatem amicus erat Miloni, egisse quoque dicebatur ne se de hac re consulendo invidia oneraret.

Inter haec cum crebresceret rumor Cn. Pompeium

brother, C. Claudius, and were investigating their uncle's death as it were in their father's name.) Two others, Valerius Nepos and Valerius Leo, also lodged summonses against Milo's and Fausta's *familiae.* In addition L. Herennius Balbus summoned Clodius' *familia* and associates, and Caelius did the same with that of Hypsaeus and Q. Pompeius. The following spoke for Milo: Q. Hortensius, M. Cicero, M. Marcellus, M. Calidius, M. Cato, Faustus Sulla. Hortensius gave a brief address, saying that those being summoned like slaves were in fact free men, since Milo had emancipated them after the recent fatal incident for saving his life. All this took place during the intercalary month.[3]

About 30 days after Clodius' death Q. Metellus Scipio clashed with Q. Caepio in the senate on the matter of this death. He alleged that Milo's defence had been a lie, and that Clodius had set out to address the officials of Aricia with 26 slaves; that after the senate had risen *(35)* Milo had suddenly gone at 10 a.m. to intercept him with over 300 armed slaves, and had caught him off guard on the way above Bovillae; that Clodius had been wounded three times and carried into Bovillae; Milo had stormed the inn in which he had taken refuge, and Clodius had been dragged out scarcely alive, killed on the Appian Way, and his ring removed. Then, said Metellus, Milo had arrived at a house in the neighbourhood of Alba, knowing that Clodius' young son was staying there; as the boy had already been moved, Milo interrogated the slave, Halicor, by severing his limbs one by one, and strangled the foreman and two other slaves as well. Eleven of the slaves protecting Clodius had lost their lives, while only two of Milo's had been injured; the next day Milo had freed 12 slaves who had done him particular service there, and had distributed 1000 *asses* to each of the tribal voters to help suppress the rumours about him. It was claimed that Milo had informed Pompey, who strongly supported his quaestor Hypsaeus, that he would abandon his consular campaign if Pompey wished it; but that Pompey replied that he did not induce anyone to stand or not to stand, and would not infringe the discretion of the Roman *populus* by offering advice or opinion. Then he apparently took steps through C. Lucilius, a friend of Milo because of his attachment to Cicero, to see that he did not attract unpopularity over this negotiation.

During all this time public feeling was growing that

creari dictatorem oportere neque aliter mala civitatis sedari posse, *(36)* visum est optimatibus tutius esse eum consulem sine collega creari, et cum tractata ea res esset in senatu, facto in M. Bibuli sententiam S.C. Pompeius ab interrege Servio Sulpicio V Kal. Mart. mense intercalario consul creatus est statimque consulatum iniit.

Deinde post diem tertium de legibus novis ferendis rettulit: duas ex S.C. promulgavit, alteram de vi qua nominatim caedem in Appia via factam et incendium curiae et domum M. Lepidi interregis oppugnatam comprehendit, alteram de ambitu: poena graviore et forma iudiciorum breviore. Vtraque enim lex prius testes dari, deinde uno die atque eodem et ab accusatore et a reo perorari iubebat, ita ut duae horae accusatori, tres reo darentur.

His legibus obsistere M. Caelius tr.pl. studiosissimus Milonis conatus est, quod et privilegium diceret in Milonem ferri et iudicia praecipitari. Et cum pertinacius leges Caelius vituperaret, eo processit irae Pompeius ut diceret, si coactus esset, armis se rem publicam defensurum. Timebat autem Pompeius Milonem seu timere se simulabat: plerumque non domi suae sed in hortis manebat, idque ipsum in superioribus circa quos etiam magna manus militum excubabat. Senatum quoque semel repente dimiserat Pompeius, quod diceret timere se adventum Milonis.

Dein proximo senatu P. Cornificius ferrum Milonem intra tunicam habere ad femur alligatum dixerat; postulaverat ut femur nudaret, et ille sine mora tunicam levarat: tum M. Cicero exclamaverat omnia illi similia crimina esse quae in Milonem dicerentur alia.

(37) Deinde T. Munatius Plancus tribunus plebis produxerat in contionem M. Aemilium Philemonem, notum hominem, libertum M. Lepidi. Is se dicebat pariterque secum quattuor liberos homines iter facientes supervenisse cum Clodius occideretur, et ob id cum proclamassent, abreptos et perductos per duos menses in villa Milonis praeclusos fuisse; eaque res seu vera seu falsa magnam invidiam Miloni contraxerat. Idem quoque Munatius et Pompeius tribuni plebis in rostra produxerant triumvirum capitalem, eumque interrogaverant an Galatam Milonis servum caedes facientem deprehendisset. Ille

Pompey should be appointed *dictator*, as the only way to solve the country's problems; *(36)* so the *optimates* thought it safer for him to be made consul without a colleague. The senate debated the question, and then on the 24th (?) of the intercalary month[3] a senatorial decree was passed on the motion of M. Bibulus, and Pompey was made consul by the *interrex* Servius Sulpicius and at once took up office. Three days later he proposed fresh legislation, and published two bills arising out of a senatorial decree: one concerned violence, and specifically mentioned the death on the Appian Way, the destruction of the senate-house, and the assault on the home of the *interrex* M. Lepidus; the second dealt with bribery. Enhanced penalties and a shorter form of legal procedure were laid down. Each bill prescribed that witnesses should be produced first, then that both prosecutor and defendant should complete their speeches in a single day, two hours being allowed to the prosecutor, three to the defendant. The *tribunus plebis* M. Caelius, a staunch supporter of Milo, tried to resist these bills, asserting that they were a personal attack on Milo and were undermining the position of the courts. Caelius persisted in his objections, and Pompey grew so angry that he said he would defend the state with force if it became necessary. In fact, Pompey was afraid of Milo, or pretended that he was; he tended to stay in his garden villa, and even so he used the upper part of it, with a large troop of soldiers to keep watch. On one occasion he abruptly ended a meeting of the senate, saying he was afraid of Milo's arrival. At the next meeting, P. Cornificius alleged that Milo had a sword inside his tunic strapped to his thigh; he called for him to bare his thigh, and Milo at once lifted his tunic. M. Cicero remarked then that this allegation was typical of those made against Milo. *(37)* After this the *tribunus plebis* T. Munatius Plancus brought a well-known freedman of M. Lepidus called M. Aemilius Philemon to a *contio*: he said that he and four free persons had been travelling when they came upon the murder of Clodius; they had protested, and been seized and abducted, then imprisoned for two months in a house belonging to Milo. Whether this story was true or false, it caused much feeling against Milo. In addition Munatius and Pompeius, another *tribunus plebis*, brought a *triumvir capitalis* to the platform and asked him if he had arrested Galata, Milo's slave, in the act of murder.

dormientem in taberna pro fugitivo prehensum et ad se perductum esse responderat. Denuntiaverant tamen triumviro, ne servum remitteret: sed postera die Caelius tribunus plebis et Manilius Cumanus collega eius ereptum e domo triumviri servum Miloni reddiderant. Haec, etsi nullam de his criminibus mentionem fecit Cicero, tamen, quia ita compereram, putavi exponenda. Inter primos et Q. Pompeius et C. Sallustius et T. Munatius Plancus tribuni plebis inimicissimas contiones de Milone habebant, invidiosas etiam de Cicerone, quod Milonem tanto studio defenderet. Eratque maxima pars multitudinis infensa non solum Miloni sed etiam propter invisum patrocinium Ciceroni. Postea Pompeius et Sallustius in suspicione fuerunt redisse in gratiam cum Milone ac Cicerone; Plancus autem infestissime perstitit, atque in Ciceronem *(38)* quoque multitudinem instigavit. Pompeio autem suspectum faciebat Milonem, ad perniciem eius comparari vim vociferatus: Pompeiusque ob ea saepius querebatur sibi quoque fieri insidias et id palam, ac maiore manu se armabat. Dicturum quoque diem Ciceroni Plancus ostendebat postea, ante Q. Pompeius idem meditatus erat. Tanta tamen constantia ac fides fuit Ciceronis ut non populi a se alienatione, non Cn. Pompeii suspicionibus, non periculo futurum ut sibi dies ad populum diceretur, non armis quae palam in Milonem sumpta erant deterreri potuerit a defensione eius: cum posset omne periculum suum et offensionem inimicae multitudinis declinare, redimere autem Cn. Pompeii animum, si paulum ex studio defensionis remisisset.

Perlata deinde lege Pompei, in qua id quoque scriptum erat ut quaesitor suffragio populi ex iis qui consules fuerant crearetur, statim comitia habita, creatusque est L. Domitius Ahenobarbus quaesitor. Album quoque iudicum qui de ea re iudicarent Pompeius tale proposuit ut numquam neque clariores viros neque sanctiores propositos esse constaret. Post quod statim nova lege Milo postulatus est a duobus Appiis Claudiis adulescentibus iisdem a quibus antea familia eius fuerat postulata; itemque de ambitu ab iisdem Appiis, et praeterea a C. Ateio et L. Cornificio; de sodaliciis etiam *(39)* a P. Fulvio Nerato. Postulatus autem erat et de sodaliciis et de ambitu ea spe, quod primum iudicium de vi futurum apparebat, quo eum damnatum iri confidebant nec postea responsurum.

His reply was that the man had been caught while asleep in the inn like a runaway, and had been brought to him. They instructed the *triumvir* not to release the slave, but next day the *tribunus plebis* Caelius and his colleague Manilius Cumanus took the slave from the *triumvir's* house and returned him to Milo. Now although none of these stories appears in Cicero's speech, I thought I should set out my discoveries.

The *tribuni plebis* Q. Pompeius, C. Sallustius, and T. Munatius held particularly hostile *contiones* aimed at Milo, critical of Cicero too, since he was so energetic in Milo's defence. Indeed most of the masses hated Milo, and Cicero because of his objectionable patronage of him. Later on, Pompeius and Sallustius were suspected of being reconciled with Milo and Cicero, but Plancus maintained his hostility and provoked the masses against him. *(38)* He also caused suspicion of Milo in Pompey, saying that Pompey's downfall was being plotted by force. Pompey began complaining frequently that traps were being set for him, and increased his armed guard. Plancus claimed that he was going to prosecute Cicero soon, something earlier contemplated by Q. Pompeius. However, Cicero showed the greatest loyalty and resolve, saying that he could not be deterred from defending Milo by either the popular discontent, or Pompey's suspicions, or the danger of prosecution, or the open organizing of violence against Milo; he could after all shrug off any danger to himself and unpopularity with the masses, and reclaim Pompey's favour too, if he put a little less energy into Milo's defence.

Pompey's bill passed into law, including a clause providing that a *quaesitor* of the vote of the *populus* should be appointed from the ex-consuls; immediately the elections were over, L. Domitius Ahenobarbus was appointed to this position. Further, Pompey put forward a panel of jurors for this purpose of an unparalleled distinction and soundness. At once Milo was summoned under the new law by the young Appii Claudii who had previously summoned his *familia*; a charge of bribery was also preferred by the Appii, and by C. Ateius and L. Cornificius, and one of unlawful association by P. Fulvius Neratus. *(39)* The motive of these last two charges was that since the charge of violence was bound to be heard first, they felt confident that he would be convicted on that, and would not therefore appear to defend himself on

Divinatio de ambitu accusatorum facta est quaesitore A. Torquato, atque ambo quaesitores, Torquatus et Domitius, prid. Non. April. reum adesse iusserunt. Quo die Milo ad Domiti tribunal venit, ad Torquati amicos misit; ibi postulante pro eo M. Marcello obtinuit ne prius causam de ambitu diceret quam de vi iudicium esset perfectum.

Apud Domitium autem quaesitorem maior Appius postulavit a Milone servos exhiberi numero IIII et L, et cum ille negaret eos qui nominabantur in sua potestate esse, Domitius ex sententia iudicum pronuntiavit ut ex servorum suorum numero accusator quot vellet ederet.

Citati deinde testes secundum legem quae, ut supra diximus, iubebat ut prius quam causa ageretur testes per triduum audirentur, dicta eorum iudices consignarent, quarta die adesse omnes iuberentur ac coram accusatore ac reo pilae in quibus nomina iudicum inscripta essent aequarentur; dein rursus postera die sortitio iudicum fieret unius et LXXX: qui numerus cum sorte obtigisset, ipsi protinus sessum irent; tum ad dicendum accusator duas horas, reus tres haberet, resque eodem die illo iudicaretur; prius autem quam sententiae ferrentur, quinos ex singulis ordinibus accusator, totidem reus reiceret, ita ut numerus iudicum relinqueretur qui sententias ferrent quinquaginta et unus.

(40) Primo die datus erat in Milonem testis C. Causinius Schola, qui se cum P. Clodio fuisse, cum is occisus esset, dixit, atrocitatemque rei factae quam maxime potuit auxit. Quem cum interrogare M. Marcellus coepisset, tanto tumultu Clodianae multitudinis circumstantis exterritus est ut vim ultimam timens in tribunal a Domitio reciperetur. Quam ob causam Marcellus et ipse Milo a Domitio praesidium imploraverunt.

Sedebat eo tempore Cn. Pompeius ad aerarium, perturbatusque erat eodem illo clamore: itaque Domitio promisit se postero die cum praesidio descensurum, idque fecit. Qua re territi Clodiani silentio verba testium per biduum audiri passi sunt. Interrogaverunt eos M. Cicero et M. Marcellus et Milo ipse. Multi ex iis qui Bovillis habitabant testimonium dixerunt de eis quae ibi facta erant: coponem occisum, tabernam expugnatam, corpus Clodi in publicum extractum esse.

the others.

Then came a hearing to decide which accuser should bring the charge of bribery, the *quaesitor* being A. Torquatus; and both *quaesitores*, Torquatus and Domitius, ordered the accused to appear on 4 April. On that day Milo attended Domitius' court, and sent friends to represent him before Torquatus. At the latter an application on his behalf by M. Marcellus was granted – that he need not answer the charge of bribery until the trial for violence was over. The elder Appius applied to Domitius to have 54 of Milo's slaves brought to court; Milo objected that the persons named were not in his possession; Domitius ruled that the plaintiff might produce as many of these slaves as he wished. The witnesses were then summoned in accordance with the law (mentioned earlier), under which witnesses were to be heard for three days before the case began, and their statements certified by the jury. On the fourth day they were all to attend again, so that, in the presence of the plaintiff and defendant, the balls with a juryman's name inscribed on each could be checked for equal weight and shape. The following day 81 jurymen were to be selected by lot, and these should take their seats forthwith; the plaintiff was to be allowed two hours and the defendant three to state their cases, and the verdict would be declared the same day. However, before that last stage was reached, the plaintiff and defendant might each reject five jurors from each social rank,[4] leaving 51 to produce the verdict.

(40) On the first day C. Causinius Schola appeared as prosecution witness; he stated that he had been with Clodius at the time of his death, and proceeded to enhance the horror of that event as much as he could. M. Marcellus began to question him, but was so frightened by the uproar from the Clodius gang which was standing around that he sought protection from Domitius on the platform in fear of extreme violence. Then both Marcellus and Milo asked Domitius for armed assistance. At the time Pompey was encamped near the treasury building, and the uproar worried him too; so he assured Domitius that he would arrive next day with an armed guard, which he did. This subdued the Clodians, and for two days they allowed the witnesses to be heard in silence; the questioning was conducted by Cicero, M. Marcellus, and Milo himself. Several inhabitants of Bovillae gave evidence about the events there – the death of the innkeeper, the

Virgines quoque Albanae dixerunt mulierem ignotam venisse ad se quae Milonis mandato votum solveret, quod Clodius occisus esset.

Vltimae testimonium dixerunt Sempronia, Tuditani filia, socrus P. Clodi, et uxor Fulvia, et fletu suo magnopere eos qui assistebant commoverunt. Dimisso circa horam decimam iudicio T. Munatius pro contione populum adhortatus est ut postero die frequens adesset et elabi Milonem non paterentur, iudiciumque et dolorem suum ostenderet euntibus ad tabellam ferendam. Postero die, qui fuit iudicii summus a.d. VII *(41)* Idus Aprilis, clausae fuerunt tota urbe tabernae; praesidia in foro et circa omnis fori aditus Pompeius disposuit; ipse pro aerario, ut pridie, consedit saeptus delecta manu militum. Sortitio deinde iudicum a prima die facta est: post tantum silentium toto foro fuit quantum esse in aliquo foro posset. Tum intra horam secundam accusatores coeperunt dicere Appius maior et M. Antonius et P. Valerius Nepos. Vsi sunt ex lege horis duabus.

Respondit his unus M. Cicero: et cum quibusdam placuisset ita defendi crimen, interfici Clodium pro re publica fuisse - quam formam M. Brutus secutus est in ea oratione quam pro Milone composuit et edidit quasi egisset - Ciceroni id non placuit ut, quisquis bono publico damnari, idem etiam occidi indemnatus posset. Itaque cum insidias Milonem Clodio fecisse posuissent accusatores, quia falsum id erat - nam forte illa rixa commissa fuerat - Cicero apprehendit et contra Clodium Miloni fecisse insidias disputavit, eoque tota oratio eius spectavit. Sed ita constitit ut diximus, nec utrius consilio pugnatum esse eo die, verum et forte occurrisse et ex rixa servorum ad eam denique caedem perventum. Notum tamen erat utrumque mortem alteri saepe minatum esse, et sicut suspectum Milonem maior quam Clodi familia faciebat, ita expeditior et paratior ad pugnam Clodianorum quam Milonis fuerat.

Cicero cum inciperet dicere, exceptus est acclamatione Clodianorum, qui se continere ne metu quidem circum-stantium *(42)* militum potuerunt. Itaque non ea qua solitus erat constantia dixit. Manet autem illa quoque excepta eius oratio: scripsit vero hanc quam legimus ita perfecte ut iure prima haberi possit.

assault on the inn, and the hauling out of Clodius' body.
Then some virgins from Alba stated that an unknown
woman had come to them on Milo's instructions to give
thanks for the death of Clodius. Finally Sempronia,
daughter of Tuditanus and mother-in-law of Clodius, and
Clodius' wife Fulvia created much emotion among the
onlookers with their tears. The court adjourned at about
4 p.m., and then T. Munatius held a *contio* and urged the
populus to turn up the next day in a mass and not let
Milo get away; they were to show their attitude to the
case to the jurors as they presented their votes. The
next day, 7 April, the last day of the trial, *(41)* all the
city inns were closed; Pompey posted guards in the forum
and all its approaches, and waited himself as before, next
to the treasury, fenced around by selected troops. The
jurors were selected by lot, and then silence fell in the
forum, at least as much as there ever can be in such
places. Shortly after 8 a.m. the prosecutors, the elder
Appius, M. Antonius, P. Valerius Nepos, began their case,
using the two hours allowed by the law.

For the defence Cicero alone appeared: some thought
the best defence was that Clodius' murder was in the
public interest (in fact M. Brutus used this line of
argument in the speech he wrote for Milo and published
as if he had delivered it), but Cicero took a different
view; he did not believe that a man whose conviction
would be in the public interest could fairly be put to
death without being convicted. The prosecution had
claimed that Milo had ambushed Clodius (falsely of course
– the fight had occurred by pure chance); Cicero took
this up and argued that it was Clodius who had ambushed
Milo; indeed he made this the whole burden of his speech.
In actual fact the incident happened as I have described:
the fight was not the deliberate intention of either man,
but had occurred by chance, starting with a brawl among
the slaves and ending with the killing. It was well known
that they had often threatened each other with death;
and while suspicion fell on Milo because of his larger
familia, Clodius' followers had been less encumbered and
readier for a fight.

Cicero began his speech, and was greeted with uproar
from the Clodians, since even the fear of the soldiers did
not inhibit them. *(42)* As a result he spoke without his
usual firmness of purpose. The speech he gave has
actually survived, but the one we are concerned with at

E N A R R A T I O

VERS. A PRIMO L

[§3] *Vnum genus est adversum infestumque nobis* et
cetera.

Ita ut in causae expositione diximus, Munatius Plancus
pridie pro contione populum adhortatus erat ne pateretur
elabi Milonem.

VER. A PRIMO CC

[§12] *Declarant huius ambusti tribuni plebis illae
intermortuae contiones quibus cotidie meam potentiam
invidiose criminabatur.*

T. Munatius Plancus et Q. Pompeius Rufus tribuni pl.,
de quibus in argumento huius orationis diximus, cum
contra Milonem Scipioni et Hypsaeo studerent, contionati
sunt eo ipso tempore plebemque in Milonem accenderunt
quo propter Clodi corpus curia incensa est, nec prius
destiterunt quam flamma eius incendii fugati sunt e
contione. Erant enim tunc rostra non eo loco quo nunc
sunt sed ad comitium, prope iuncta curiae. Ob hoc T.
Munatium *ambustum tribunum* appellat; fuit autem paratus
ad dicendum.

PAVLO POST

[§13] *Cur igitur incendium curiae, oppugnationem (43)
aedium M. Lepidi, caedem hanc ipsam contra rem publicam
senatus factam esse decrevit?*

Post biduum medium quam Clodius occisus erat interrex primus proditus est M. Aemilius Lepidus. Non fuit
autem moris ab eo qui primus interrex proditus erat
comitia haberi. Sed Scipionis et Hypsaei factiones, quia
recens invidia Milonis erat, cum contra ius postularent ut
interrex ad comitia consulum creandorum descenderet,
idque ipse non faceret, domum eius per omnes interregni
dies – fuerunt autem ex more quinque – obsederunt.
Deinde omni vi ianua expugnata et imagines maiorum

present is such a masterpiece that it can rightly be called supreme.[5]

COMMENTARY

(about 50 lines from the start)
[§3] *Our opponents and those hostile to us form one single group* etc.

As I explained in the *Exposition* above, the previous day Munatius Plancus had addressed a *contio* of the *populus* and urged them not to allow Milo to get away.

(about 200 lines from the start)
[§12] *That is made abundantly clear by the moribund contiones of that somewhat scorched tribunus plebis, those in which he daily and with malice impugned my authority.*

The *tribuni plebis* T. Munatius Plancus and Q. Pompeius Rufus, whom I have already mentioned in the *Exposition*, supported Scipio and Hypsaeus against Milo; at exactly this stage they addressed a *contio* and incited the *plebs* against Milo. The senate-house then caught fire along with Clodius' body, yet they continued to speak until they were driven away by the flames. The platform was not then in its present position, but near the assembly-place almost beside the senate-house. Hence he calls Munatius a "somewhat scorched *tribunus plebis*", as he was so eager an orator.

(shortly afterwards)
[§13] *Why then did the senate determine that the destruction of the senate-house, (43) the assault on Lepidus' home, this fatal incident itself, were contrary to the public interest?*

Roughly two days after the death of Clodius, M. Aemilius Lepidus was appointed the first *interrex*. It was not the practice for the first man so appointed to hold elections; but Scipio and Hypsaeus' supporters, enjoying Milo's new unpopularity, broke this tradition and demanded that the *interrex* should embark on consular elections. Lepidus did not do so, and they kept his house surrounded throughout the period (as usual five days) of his interregnum. After this they broke down the door with great violence, overturned the busts of his ancestors, and smashed a sofa which was in the way,

deiecerunt et lectulum adversum uxoris eius Corneliae, cuius castitas pro exemplo habita est, fregerunt, iterumque telas quae ex vetere more in atrio texebantur diruerunt. Post quae supervenit Milonis manus et ipsa postulans comitia; cuius adventus fuit saluti Lepido: in se enim ipsae conversae sunt factiones inimicae, atque ita oppugnatio domus interregis omissa est.

PAVLO POST

[§14] *Quod si per furiosum illum tribunum pl. senatui quod sentiebat perficere licuisset, novam quaestionem nullam haberemus. Decernebat enim ut veteribus legibus, tantum modo extra ordinem, quaereretur. Divisa sententia est postulante nescio quo. Sic reliqua auctoritas senatus empta intercessione sublata est.*

Quid sit dividere sententiam ut enarrandum sit vestra aetas, filii, facit.

Cum aliquis in dicenda sententia duas pluresve res complectitur, *(44)* si non omnes eae probantur, postulatur ut dividatur, id est de rebus singulis referatur. Forsitan nunc hoc quoque velitis scire qui fuerit qui id postu- laverit. Quod non fere adicitur: non enim ei qui hoc postulat oratione longa utendum ac ne consurgendum quidem utique est; multi enim sedentes hoc unum verbum pronuntiant *Divide*: quod cum auditum est, liberum est ei qui facit relationem dividere. Sed ego, ut curiosius aetati vestrae satisfaciam, Acta etiam totius illius temporis persecutus sum; in quibus cognovi pridie Kal. Mart. S.C. esse factum, P. Clodi caedem et incendium curiae et oppugantionem aedium M. Lepidi contra rem p. factam; ultra relatum in Actis illo die nihil; postero die, id est Kal. Mart., T. Munatium in contione exposuisse populo quae pridie acta erant in senatu: in qua contione haec dixit ad verbum.

Cum Hortensius dixisset ut extra ordinem quaereretur apud quaesitorem; existimaret futurum ut, cum pusillum dedisset dulcedinis, largiter acerbitatis devorarent: adversus hominem ingeniosum nostro ingenio usi sumus; invenimus Fufium, qui diceret "Divide"; reliquae parti sententiae (45) ego et Sallustius intercessimus.

belonging to his wife Cornelia, an utterly respectable lady; they also destroyed the looms which were being worked in the hall according to the old custom. At this point Milo's group arrived, also calling for elections, and saved Lepidus, since the two opposed gangs turned on each other and the assault on the *interrex*'s house ceased.

(shortly afterwards)

[§14] *Now if the senate had been allowed by that demented* tribunus plebis *to take the steps it intended, we should not be now holding a new form of investigation. It was going to decide that it should be conducted under the existing rules, although with special precedence. But a vote was called on someone's insistence. So the remainder of the senate's resolution was lost by a corrupt veto.*

Your age, my boys, makes it necessary to explain what "calling a vote" means.

Suppose someone makes a speech covering two or more issues: *(44)* if the opinions do not all gain approval, a vote is called, that is each is considered separately. You may wish to know who called on that occasion; however, it is not normal to make a note of his name; a man who calls need not speak at length or even get to his feet. A number of men may simply shout one word "*divide*" from their seats, and when he hears this, the proposer may go ahead with the vote. However, I decided to take a little more trouble to satisfy your young inquiring minds, so I have gone through the *Acta* for the whole period. I have discovered a decree of the senate, dated 28 February, to the effect that the killing of Clodius, the destruction of the senate-house, and the assault on Lepidus' house were contrary to the public interest; apart from the motion, there is nothing in the *Acta* for that day. But next day, 1 March, T. Munatius is recorded as describing at a *contio* the senate's proceedings of the previous day; the following is a transcript:

> Hortensius has suggested an inquiry with special priority before a *quaesitor*: no doubt he thought that if offered an attractive morsel, they would greedily swallow what was distasteful.[6] Against an ingenious man we have employed our own ingenuity: we have engaged Fufius to call a vote, *(45)* and the rest of

Haec contio, ut puto, explicat et quid senatus decernere voluerit, et quis divisionem postulaverit, et quis intercesserit et cur. Illud vos meminisse non dubito per Q. Fufium illo quoque tempore quo de incesto P. Clodi actum est factum ne a senatu asperius decerneretur.

De L. Domitio dicit:
[§22] *Dederas enim quam contemneres populares insanias iam ab adulescentia documenta maxima.*

Constantiam L. Domiti quam in quaestura praestitit significat. Nam eo tempore cum M. Manilius tribunus plebis subnixus libertinorum et servorum manu perditissimam legem ferret ut libertinis in omnibus tribubus suffragium esset, idque per tumultum ageret et clivum Capitolium obsideret, discusserat perruperatque coetum Domitius ita ut multi Manilianorum occiderentur. Quo facto et plebem infimam offenderat et senatus magnam gratiam inierat.

[§32] *Itaque illud Cassianum indicium in his personis valeat.*

L. Cassius fuit, sicut iam saepe diximus, summae vir severitatis. Is quotiens quaesitor iudicii alicuius esset in quo quaerebatur de homine occiso suadebat atque etiam praeibat iudicibus hoc quod Cicero nunc admonet, ut quaereretur cui bono fuisset perire eum de cuius morte quaeritur.

Ob quam severitatem, quo tempore Sex. Peducaeus tribunus plebis criminatus est L. Metellum pontificem max. totumque *(46)* collegium pontificum male iudicasse de incesto virginum Vestalium, quod unam modo Aemiliam damnaverat, absolverat autem duas Marciam et Liciniam, populus hunc Cassium creavit qui de eisdem virginibus quaereret. Isque et utrasque eas et praeterea complures alias nimia etiam, ut existimatio est, asperitate usus damnavit.

[§33] *Et aspexit me illis quidem oculis quibus tunc solebat cum omnibus omnia minabatur. Movet me quippe !umen curiae!*

Hic est Sex. Clodius quem in argumento huius orationis diximus corpus Clodi in curiam intulisse et ibi

the proposal has been vetoed by Sallustius and myself.
I think that this address shows what the senate intended to decree, who called the vote, who placed the veto, and why. I am sure too that you remember (≠) that this Q. Fufius ensured, at the time when the case of Clodius' breach of religious law was discussed, that the senate's decree was not too stringent.

Cicero says this about L. Domitius:
[§22] *Ever since your youth you gave ample evidence of your contempt for the follies of* populares.
He is referring to the firmness shown by Domitius in his quaestorship. At the time *(67/6 B.C.)* the *tribunus plebis* C. Manilius, supported by a squad of freedmen and slaves, was proposing a deplorable bill to distribute freedmen's votes throughout the tribes; there was some disturbance, and Manilius occupied the Capitoline Hill. Then Domitius broke up this gang with many deaths among Manilius' supporters. This deed antagonized the mob and gave Domitius much prestige in the senate.

[§32] *So let Cassius' test be applied in the case of these characters.*
I have often remarked (≠) that L. Cassius was a thoroughly stern figure. Whenever he was presiding in court over a case of homicide, he used to give the advice, indeed the instruction, applied here by Cicero: the jury should ask in whose interest was the death of the man in question. Now there was the occasion *(113 B.C.)* when Sex. Peducaeus accused the chief priest L. Metellus and the whole pontifical college *(46)* of delivering an unsound verdict in the case of the incest of the Vestal Virgins (they had convicted Aemilia alone, and acquitted Marcia and Licinia); so because of his reputation for sternness Cassius was appointed by the *populus* to investigate the Vestals. He convicted the two mentioned and several others also – a piece of perhaps excessive severity.

[§33] *And he has used upon me that stare which he employed when delivering his comprehensive threats then on everyone. How I am impressed by that glare from the senate-house!*
This man, Sex. Cloelius, as I said in the *Exposition*, brought Clodius' body into the senate-house, cremated it

cremasse eoque incenso curiam conflagrasse; ideo *lumen curiae* dicit.

[§37] *Quando illius postea sica illa quam a Catilina acceperat conquievit? Haec intenta nobis est, huic ego obici vos pro me passus non sum, haec insidiata Pompeio est.*

Haec intenta nobis est et *obici vos pro me non sum passus,* manifestum est pertinere ad id tempus quo post rogationem a P. Clodio in eum promulgatam urbe cessit. Qua re dicat *insidiata Pompeio est* fortassis quaeratis.

Pisone et Gabinio coss. pulso Cicerone in exsilium, cum III Idus Sextiles Pompeius in senatum venit, dicitur servo P. Clodi sica excidisse, eaque ad Gabinium consulem delata dictum est servo imperatum a P. Clodio ut Pompeius occideretur.

Pompeius statim domum rediit et ex eo domi se tenuit. Obsessus est etiam a liberto *(47)* Clodi Damione, ut ex Actis eius anni cognovi, in quibus XV Kal. Sept. L. Novius tribunus plebis, collega Clodi, cum Damio adversum L. Flavium praetorem appellaret tribunos et tribuni de appellatione cognoscerent, ita sententiam dixit:

Et si ab hoc apparitore P. Clodi vulneratus sum, et hominibus armatis praesidiis dispositis a re publica remotus Cn. Pompeius obsessusque est, cum appeller, non utar eius exemplo quem vitupero et iudicium tollam,

et reliqua de intercessione.

Haec viam Appiam monumentum nominis sui nece Papiri cruentavit.
Pompeius post triumphum Mithridaticum Tigranis filium in catenis deposuerat apud Flavium senatorem: qui postea cum esset praetor eodem anno quo tribunus plebis Clodius, petiit ab eo Clodius super cenam ut Tigranem adduci iuberet ut eum videret. Adductum collocavit in convivio, dein Flavio non reddidit Tigranem; domum misit et habuit extra catenas nec repetenti Pompeio reddidit.

Postea in navem deposuit, et cum profugeret ille,

there, and so burnt down the building; hence the phrase
"glare from the senate-house".

[§37] *When after that did the dagger he received from
Catilina rest unused? It is that which has been brandished at me, it is that to which I have not permitted you
all to be exposed, it is that which lay in ambush for
Pompey.*

"It is that which has been . . . exposed" clearly
refers to the time of the publication of Clodius' proposal
directed against him, when he withdrew from the city.
You may wonder what he means by "lay in ambush for
Pompey": after Cicero's expulsion in the consulship of
Piso and Gabinius *(58 B.C.)*, Pompey entered the senate on
11 August; then apparently a slave of Clodius dropped a
dagger. It was taken to the consul Gabinius, and it seems
the slave had been instructed by Clodius to kill Pompey.
Pompey immediately went home and stayed there from
then on; and according to the *Acta* for the year he was
assailed by Clodius' freedman Damio. *(47)* The *Acta* say
that on 18 August Damio appealed to the *tribuni plebis*
against the praetor L. Flavius, and while the *tribuni
plebis* were considering the appeal, a colleague of Clodius,
the *tribunus plebis* L. Novius, stated as follows:

> Even if it is true that I have been injured by this
> henchman of Clodius, and that Pompey is shut away
> from public life with his men armed and guards
> posted, and that he is under siege, in response to
> this appeal I will not use the precedent of a man I
> detest: I therefore dismiss this case;

and he went on to discuss the veto.

*It is that which has stained with the blood of
Papirius the Appian Way which bears its user's name.*

After his triumph over Mithridates Pompey had lodged
the son of Tigranes in chains at the house of the senator
Flavius; this Flavius was later on praetor in the same
year as Clodius was *tribunus plebis (58 B.C.)*, and was
asked by Clodius at dinner to have Tigranes brought
along for him to see. Tigranes was produced, installed at
the dinner, and then not returned by Clodius to Flavius.
Instead Clodius sent him to his house to be kept
unfettered, and when Pompey demanded his return he
still would not surrender him. Later on he put Tigranes
on board ship, in which the latter tried to escape, but

tempestate delatus est Antium. Inde ut deduceretur ad se,
Clodius Sex. Clodium, de quo supra diximus, misit. Qui cum
reduceret, Flavius quoque re cognita ad eripiendum
Tigranem profectus est. Ad quartum lapidem ab urbe
pugna facta est in qua multi ex utraque ceciderunt,
plures tamen ex Flavi, inter quos et M. Papirius eques
Romanus, publicanus, familiaris Pompeio. Flavius sine
comite Romam vix perfugit.

*(48) Haec eadem longo intervallo conversa rursus est
in me: nuper quidem, ut scitis, me ad Regiam paene
confecit.*

Quo die periculum hoc adierit, ut Clodius eum ad
Regiam paene confecerit, nusquam inveni; non tamen
adducor ut putem Ciceronem mentitum, praesertim cum
adiciat *ut scitis.* Sed videtur mihi loqui de eo die quo
consulibus Domitio et Messala qui praecesserant eum
annum cum haec oratio dicta est inter candidatorum
Hypsaei et Milonis manus in via Sacra pugnatum est,
multique ex Milonianis ex improviso ceciderunt. De cuius
diei periculo suo ut putem loqui eum facit et locus pugnae
– nam in Sacra via traditur commissa, in qua est Regia –
et quod adsidue simul erant cum candidatis suffragatores,
Milonis Cicero, Hypsaei Clodius.

[§38] *Potuitne L. Caecili, iustissimi fortissimique prae-
toris, obpugnata domo?*

L. Caecilius Rufus de quo dicitur fuit praetor P.
Lentulo Spinthere Q. Metello Nepote coss., quo anno Cicero
restitutus est. Is cum faceret ludos Apollinares, ita infima
coacta multitudo annonae caritate tumultuata est ut omnes
qui in theatro spectandi causa consederant pellerentur. De
oppugnata domo nusquam adhuc legi; Pompeius tamen cum
defenderet Milonem apud populum, de vi accusante Clodio,
obiecit ei, ut legimus apud Tironem libertum Ciceronis in
libro IIII de vita eius, oppressum L. Caecilium praetorem.

was driven by a storm into Antium. Clodius then sent Sex. Cloelius, mentioned earlier, to have him brought back. While they were on their way back, Flavius got to hear, and set out to seize Tigranes himself. There was a fight four miles outside Rome, with many casualties on both sides, but more on Flavius': among these was M. Papirius, an *eques*, tax-company member, and associate of Pompey. Flavius just managed to get back to Rome alone.

(48) It is that which was once again turned against me a long time later; indeed just recently it nearly brought my end near the Regia.

I have not discovered anywhere the day on which he faced this danger, when Clodius as you know nearly brought his end near the Regia; I am not inclined to think that Cicero made it up, especially as he adds the words "as you know". However, I believe he is referring to the occasion, during the consulship of Domitius and Messalla *(53 B.C.)* (the year before that of this speech), when there was a fight between the supporters of Hypsaeus and of Milo on the Sacred Way, and a number of Milo's men were unexpectedly killed. I feel this is the occasion he means, partly because of the location of the fight (it is supposed to have happened on the Sacred Way, where the Regia is), and because the candidates had the constant company of their supporters, Milo that of Cicero and Hypsaeus that of Clodius.

[§38] *Could he not have done so when the home of that upright and courageous praetor L. Caecilius was assaulted?*

The L. Caecilius Rufus referred to was praetor in the consulship of P. Lentulus Spinther and Q. Metellus Nepos *(57 B.C.)*, the year of Cicero's return from exile. While Caecilius was presenting the Apolline Games, a vulgar mob gathered and demonstrated against the price of corn, and all those who had taken their places in the theatre were driven out. I have not so far read any reference to the assault on his house; nevertheless, when Clodius prosecuted Milo for violence before the *populus*, and Pompey appeared for the defence, according to the freedman Tiro's biography of Cicero (book 4) Pompey attacked Clodius for the harassment of the praetor L. Caecilius.

(49) PAVLO POST

[§45] *At quo die? quo, ut ante dixi, fuit insanissima contio ab ipsius mercennario tribuno plebis concitata.*

Hoc significat eo die quo Clodius occisus est contionatum esse mercennarium eius tribunum plebis. Sunt autem contionati eo die, ut ex Actis apparet, C. Sallustius et Q. Pompeius, utrique et inimici Milonis et satis inquieti. Sed videtur mihi Q. Pompeium significare; nam eius seditiosior fuit contio.

[§46] *Dixit C. Causinius Schola Interamnanus, familiarissimus et idem comes Clodi, P. Clodium illo die in Albano mansurum fuisse.*

Hic fuit Causinius apud quem Clodius mansisse Interamnae videri volebat qua nocte deprehensus est in Caesaris domo, cum ibi in operto virgines pro populo Romano sacra facerent.

PAVLO POST

[§47] *Scitis, iudices, fuisse qui in hac rogatione suadenda diceret Milonis manu caedem esse factam, consilio vero maioris alicuius. Me videlicet latronem et sicarium abiecti homines ac perditi describebant.*

Q. Pompeius Rufus et C. Sallustius tribuni fuerunt quos significat. Hi enim primi de ea lege ferenda populum hortati *(50)* sunt et dixerunt a manu Milonis occisum esse Clodium *et cetera.*

[§49] *Atqui ut illi nocturnus adventus vitandus fuit, sic Miloni, cum insidiator esset, si illum ad urbem noctu accessurum sciebat, subsidendum et cetera.*

Via Appia est prope urbem monumentum Basili qui locus latrociniis fuit perquam infamis, quod ex aliis quoque multis intellegi potest.

[§55] *Comites Graeculi quocumque ibat, etiam cum in castra Etrusca properabat.*

Saepe obiecit Clodio Cicero socium eum coniurationis Catilinae fuisse; quam rem nunc quoque reticens ostendit. Fuerat enim opinio, ut Catilina ex urbe profugerat in castra Manli centurionis qui tum in Etruria ad Faesulas

(49) (shortly afterwards)
[§45] *But on what day was that? It was the one, as I have already said, on which there took place a frenzied* contio, *whipped up by his own paid* tribunus plebis.

He means by this that on the day of Clodius' death the *tribunus plebis* in his pay held a *contio.* The *Acta* make clear that the speakers on that day were C. Sallustius and Q. Pompeius, both being opponents of Milo and quite turbulent men: but I think he is referring to Q. Pompeius, since his *contio* was the more subversive.

[§46] *C. Causinius Schola of Interamna, a close friend and companion of Clodius, has stated that P. Clodius was intending to stay at his estate at Alba on that day.*

Clodius wanted it to be thought that he had stayed in Interamna at the house of this Causinius on the night when he was arrested in Caesar's house, the place where the virgins were performing the secret rituals for the Roman *populus.*

(shortly afterwards)
[§47] *Someone, as you gentlemen know, in the course of supporting this proposal asserted that the murder was Milo's doing, but that it was inspired by someone greater. Indeed it was I who was described as robber and cutthroat by certain vile and contemptible persons.*

He is referring to the *tribuni plebis* Q. Pompeius Rufus and C. Sallustius, since they were the first to urge the passing of that proposal, *(50)* saying that Clodius' murder was Milo's doing, and so forth.

[§49] *Now he needed to avoid arriving at night; and if Milo knew he would reach the city at night, he should have lain in wait, being presumably a conspirator.*

The monument of Basilius, on the Appian Way near the city, was notorious for robberies, a fact mentioned by many other sources.

[§55] *Greek henchmen attended him wherever he went, even when he was on his way to his outposts in Etruria.*

Cicero often taunted Clodius with his involvement in Catilina's conspiracy *(63 B.C.),* and he does so tacitly here. The story was that as Catilina was on his way from Rome to the encampment of Manlius the centurion, who was then organizing an army for him near Faesulae in

exercitum ei comparabat, Clodium subsequi eum voluisse et coepisse, tum dein mutato consilio in urbem redisse.

[§67] *Non iam hoc Clodianum crimen timemus, sed tuas, Cn. Pompei – te enim appello, et ea voce ut me exaudire possis – tuas, inquam, suspiciones perhorrescimus.*

Diximus in argumento orationis huius Cn. Pompeium simulasse timorem, seu plane timuisse Milonem, et ideo ne domi quidem suae sed in hortis superioribus ante iudicium mansisse, ita ut villam quoque praesidio militum circumdaret.

Q. Pompeius Rufus tribunus plebis, qui fuerat familiarissimus omnium P. Clodio et sectam illam sequi se *(51)* palam profitebatur, dixerat in contione paucis post diebus quam Clodius erat occisus:
Milo dedit quem in curia cremaretis: dabit quem in Capitolio sepeliatis.

In eadem contione idem dixerat – habuit enim eam a.d. VIII Kal. Febr. – cum Milo pridie, id est VIIII Kal. Febr., venire ad Pompeium in hortos eius voluisset, Pompeium ei per hominem propinquum misisse nuntium ne ad se veniret. Prius etiam quam Pompeius ter consul crearetur, tres tribuni, Q. Pompeius Rufus, C. Sallustius Crispus, T. Munatius Plancus, cum cotidianis contionibus suis magnam invidiam Miloni propter occisum Clodium excitarent, produxerant ad populum Cn. Pompeium et ab eo quaesierant num ad eum delatum esset illius quoque rei indicium, suae vitae insidiari Milonem. Responderat Pompeius: Licinium quendam de plebe sacrificulum qui solitus esset familias purgare ad se detulisse servos quosdam Milonis itemque libertos comparatos esse ad caedem suam, nomina quoque servorum edidisse; se ad Milonem misisse utrum in potestate sua haberet; a Milone responsum esse, ex iis servis quos nominasset partim neminem se umquam habuisse, partim manumisisse; dein, cum Licinium apud se haberet, . . . Lucium quendam de plebe ad corrumpendum indicem venisse; qua re cognita in vincla eum publica esse coniectum. Decreverat enim senatus ut cum interrege et tribunis plebis Pompeius daret operam ne quid res publica detrimenti caperet. Ob has suspiciones Pompeius in *(52)* superioribus hortis se continuerat; deinde ex S.C. dilectu per Italiam habito cum

Etruria, Clodius had intended following him and indeed set out, then changed his mind and returned to Rome.

[§67] *We no longer fear the charge involving Clodius' death, rather we fear your suspicions, Pompey – it is you I am now addressing, in a voice loud enough for you to hear.*

In the *Exposition* of this speech I said that Pompey pretended to be afraid of Milo, or perhaps he genuinely was. So until the verdict was given he stayed not at his house but in the upper part of his garden villa, with his residence defended by a garrison. The *tribunus plebis* Q. Pompeius Rufus, who was the closest associate of Clodius and made no secret of belonging to his clique, *(51)* had spoken at a *contio* a few days after Clodius' death as follows:

It was Milo who provided a body to be cremated in the senate-house: it is Milo who will provide one to be buried on the Capitol.

At this same *contio* on 25 January he had also said that Milo had intended visiting Pompey in his garden villa on the 24th, but Pompey had sent a message by an intimate associate telling him not to come. Even before Pompey's appointment as consul for the third time, three *tribuni plebis* – Q. Pompeius Rufus, C. Sallustius Crispus, T. Munatius Plancus – had at daily *contiones* been inflaming feeling against Milo because of Clodius' murder, and had brought Pompey before the *populus*, asking him whether he had acquired evidence that Milo was plotting against his life. Pompey's reply was that a man called Licinius, a *plebeius* priest who carried out purifications, had given him some information, namely that some slaves and freedmen of Milo's had been instructed to murder him; Licinius also named the slaves. He Pompey had inquired whether Milo had them in his jurisdiction. Milo's reply had been that of the slaves identified some had never been his property, some he had emancipated. Then, while Licinius was still with him, Pompey had had a visit from Lucius, a *plebeius*, who had come to bribe the informer. This fact came out, and the man was then imprisoned, since the senate had passed a decree that Pompey, together with the *interrex* and the *tribuni plebis*, should ensure that the state suffered no harm. Pompey had by now become suspicious, *(52)* and remained in the upper part of his garden villa. After this, troops were raised in

redisset, venientem ad se Milonem unum omnium non
admiserat. Item cum senatus in porticu Pompeii haberetur
ut Pompeius posset interesse, unum eum excuti prius
quam in senatum intraret iusserat. Hae sunt suspiciones
quas se dicit pertimescere.

[§71] *Quid enim minus illo dignum quam cogere ut vos*
eum condemnetis in quem animadvertere ipse et more
maiorum et suo iure posset? sed praesidio esse et cetera.

Idem T. Munatius Plancus, ut saepe diximus, post
audita et obsignata testium verba dimissosque interim
iudices vocata contione cohortatus erat populum ut clausis
tabernis postero die ad iudicium adesset nec pateretur
elabi Milonem.

[§87] *Incidebantur iam domi leges quae nos servis nostris*
addicerent.

Significasse iam puto nos fuisse inter leges P. Clodi
quas ferre proposuerat eam quoque qua libertini, qui non
plus quam in IIII tribubus suffragium ferebant, possent
in rusticis quoque tribubus, quae propriae ingenuorum
sunt, ferre.

[§88] *Senatus, credo, praetorem eum circumscripsisset. Ne*
cum solebat quidem id facere, in privato eodem hoc
aliquid profecerat.

Significat id tempus quo P. Clodius, cum adhuc
quaestor *(53)* designatus esset, deprensus est, cum
intrasset eo ubi sacrificium pro populo Romano fiebat.
Quod factum notatum erat . . . S.C., decretumque ut extra
ordinem de ea re iudicium fieret.

VER. A NOVIS. CLX

Quo loco inducit loquentem Milonem cum bonarum
partium hominibus de meritis suis:
[§95] *Plebem et infimam multitudinem, quae P. Clodio duce*
fortunis vestris imminebat, eam, quo tutior esset vestra
vita, se fecisse commemorat ut non modo virtute flecteret,
sed etiam tribus suis patrimoniis deleniret.

Puto iam supra esse dictum Milonem ex familia fuisse

Italy by senatorial decree, and he reappeared; of those
that called on him Milo was the only one not admitted.
Furthermore, a meeting of the senate was held in
Pompey's colonnade so that Pompey could attend, and he
insisted on Milo being removed before he would enter. So
much for the suspicions which Cicero says he fears.

[§71] *For what could be more unworthy of him than to
compel you to condemn a man whom he was empowered to
punish both by tradition and by his prerogative, but as
protection etc.*

I have said several times that T. Munatius Plancus
held a *contio*, after the witnesses were heard and attested
and the jurors asked to withdraw, during which he urged
the *populus* to shut the inns next day and attend the
court so that Milo could not get away.

[§87] *At this time laws were being engraved at his house
which would make us subject to our own slaves.*

I think I have mentioned (≠) that among Clodius'
proposed legislation there was one measure: this provided
that freedmen who hitherto voted in only four tribes
should be permitted to vote in the rural tribes also, these
being the preserve of free men.

[§88] *The senate would no doubt have limited his
activities when he became praetor! Not even when it was
in the habit of doing this had it achieved any result
when he was a private citizen.*

This is a reference to the time when Clodius, as
quaestor-elect, *(53)* had entered the place where a
sacrifice was being performed for the Roman *populus*, and
was arrested. This incident was recorded, and the senate
decreed that the case should be tried with special
priority.

(160 lines from the end)
Cicero here presents Milo discussing his services with
men of the *boni* group:
[§95] *As for that rabble, that disreputable mob, which
threatened your welfare under Clodius' leadership, he
reminds us that to promote your safety he did his utmost
not only to influence that mob by his courage but to calm
it with his three inheritances.*

I believe I stated earlier (≠) that Milo came from the

Papia, deinde adoptatum esse ab T. Annio, avo suo
materno. Tertium patrimonium videtur significare matris;
aliud enim quod fuerit non inveni.

Peracta utrimque causa singuli quinos accusator et
reus senatores, totidem equites et tribunos aerarios
reiecerunt, ita ut unus et L sententias tulerint. Senatores
condemnaverunt XII, absolverunt VI; equites condemnaverunt XIII, absolverunt IIII; tribuni aerarii condemnaverunt XIII, absolverunt III.

Videbantur non ignorasse iudices inscio Milone initio
vulneratum esse Clodium, sed compererant, post quam
vulneratus esset, iussu Milonis occisum. Fuerunt qui
crederent M. Catonis sententia eum esse absolutum; *(54)*
nam et bene cum re publica actum esse morte P. Clodi non
dissimulaverat et studebat in petitione consulatus Miloni
et reo adfuerat. Nominaverat quoque eum Cicero prae-
sentem et testatus erat audisse eum a M. Favonio ante
diem tertium quam facta caedes erat, Clodium dixisse
periturum esse eo triduo Milonem . . . Sed Milonis quoque
notam audaciam removeri a re publica utile visum est.
Scire tamen nemo umquam potuit utram sententiam
tulisset. Damnatum autem opera maxime Appi Claudi
pronuntiatum est.

Milo postero die factus reus ambitus apud Manlium
Torquatum absens damnatus est. Illa quoque lege
accusator fuit eius Appius Claudius, et cum ei praemium
lege daretur, negavit se eo uti. Subscripserunt ei in
ambitus iudicio P. Valerius Leo et Cn. Domitius Cn. f.

Post paucos dies quoque Milo apud M. Favonium
quaesitorem de sodaliciis damnatus est accusante P. Fulvio
Nerato, cui e lege praemium datum est. Deinde apud L.
Fabium quaesitorem iterum absens damnatus est de vi:
accusavit L. Cornificius et Q. Patulcius.

Milo in exsilium Massiliam intra paucissimos dies
profectus est. Bona eius propter aeris alieni magnitudinem
semuncia venierunt.

Post Milonem eadem lege Pompeia primus est accusatus
(55) M. Saufeius M. f. qui dux fuerat in expugnanda

Papius family and was adopted by T. Annius, his maternal grandfather. The third inheritance seems to be his mother's, as I have not discovered what else it can be.

When each side had finished presenting its case, both prosecutor and defendant each challenged as jurors five senators, five *equites*, and five *tribuni aerarii*; therefore 51 men voted on the verdict. 12 senators voted for conviction, 6 for acquittal; of the *equites* 13 voted for conviction, 4 for acquittal; and of the *tribuni aerarii* 13 for conviction, 3 for acquittal. It seems that the jury realized that Milo was not aware of Clodius' initial injury, but their view was that after he had been wounded he was murdered on Milo's instructions. Some people believed that M. Cato voted for acquittal, *(54)* since he openly regarded Clodius' death as a public service, and had supported Milo's campaign for the consulship and appeared for him in court. Furthermore, Cicero had specifically referred to him in his presence, and had employed his testimony that M. Favonius told him three days before the murder of Clodius' assertion that Milo would die in three days' time. . . Nevertheless, it seemed an advantage for Milo and his notoriously reckless behaviour to be banished from public life – in fact it was quite impossible to find out which side Cato had voted for.

It was mainly because of Appius Claudius' efforts that Milo was convicted. The next day Milo was charged with bribery before Manlius Torquatus and convicted in absence; in this case too he was prosecuted by Appius Claudius, who announced that he would not accept the reward provided under the law. The assistant prosecutors in the bribery case were P. Valerius Leo and Cn. Domitius son of Cnaeus.

A few days later Milo was further charged with unlawful association by P. Fulvius Neratus before the *quaesitor* M. Favonius and convicted, Neratus receiving the reward. Next he was convicted of violence, again in absence, before the *quaesitor* L. Fabius, the prosecutors being L. Cornificius and Q. Patulcius. Almost immediately Milo left for exile in Massilia; his property realized one twenty-fourth of its value owing to the size of his debts.

Other cases now ensued: the first was the prosecution of M. Saufeius son of Marcus, *(55)* under the same law of Pompey. This man had led the attack on the inn at

taberna Bovillis et Clodio occidendo. Accusaverunt eum L. Cassius, L. Fulcinius C. f., C. Valerius; defenderunt M. Cicero, M. Caelius, obtinueruntque ut una sententia absolveretur. Condemnaverunt senatores X, absolverunt VIII; condemnaverunt equites Romani VIIII, absolverunt VIII; sed ex tribunis aerariis X absolverunt, VI damnaverunt: manifestumque odium Clodi saluti Saufeio fuit, cum eius vel peior causa quam Milonis fuisset, quod aperte dux fuerat expugnandae tabernae. Repetitus deinde post paucos dies apud C. Considium quaesitorem est lege Plautia de vi, subscriptione ea quod loca edita occupasset et cum telo fuisset; nam dux fuerat operarum Milonis. Accusaverunt C. Fidius, Cn. Aponius Cn. f., M. Seius . . . Sex. f.; defenderunt M. Cicero, M. Terentius Varro Gibba. Absolutus est sententiis plenius quam prius: graves habuit XVIIII, absolutorias duas et XXX; sed e contrario hoc ac priore iudicio accidit: equites enim ac senatores eum absolverunt, tribuni aerarii damnaverunt.

Sex. autem Clodius quo auctore corpus Clodi in curiam illatum fuit accusantibus C. Caesennio Philone, M. Alfidio, defendente T. Flacconio, magno consensu damnatus est, *(56)* sententiis sex et XL; absolutorias quinque omnino habuit, duas senatorum, tres equitum.

Multi praeterea et praesentes et cum citati non respondissent damnati sunt, ex quibus maxima pars fuit Clodianorum.

Bovillae and the murder of Clodius. His prosecutors were L. Cassius, L. Fulcinius son of Caius, and C. Valerius; speakers for the defence were M. Cicero and M. Caelius. Acquittal was secured by one vote. Senators voting for conviction: 10; for acquittal: 8. *Equites* for conviction: 9; for acquittal: 8. *Tribuni aerarii* for conviction: 6; for acquittal: 10. Obviously the hostility towards Clodius helped Saufeius, since after all his defence was really weaker than Milo's, and he had undeniably led the attack on the inn. He was further charged a few days later with violence before the *quaesitor* C. Considius under the law of Plautius, with the allegation that he had been armed and had seized a commanding position, he being the leader of Milo's gang. The prosecutors were C. Fidius, Cn. Aponius son of Cnaeus, and M. Seius . . . son of Sextus; defence counsel were M. Cicero and M. Terentius Varro Gibba. This time he was acquitted more decisively, on a vote of 32 to 19; however, in one way the outcome was quite different, since now the senate and *equites* in the jury voted for acquittal, while the *tribuni aerarii* favoured conviction.

Sextus Cloelius, the man who suggested carrying Clodius' body into the senate-house, was prosecuted by C. Caesennius Philo and M. Alfidius and defended by T. Flacconius; he was overwhelmingly convicted *(56)* by a majority of 46 votes; indeed he gained only five votes for acquittal, two from the senatorial jurors, three from the *equites.*

A large number of other persons was also convicted in court, some of whom attended their trials, while others failed to answer their summonses; the majority of these were supporters of Clodius.

PRO CORNELIO

[See W. McDonald, *Classical Quarterly* 1929, pp. 196ff.; M.
T. Griffin, "The tribune C. Cornelius", *Journal of Roman
Studies* 1973, pp. 196ff.]

The year 70 B.C. was in many ways a remarkable one
politically: of the two men who served as consuls in
that year, M. Crassus was able to claim the credit for
having saved the Roman people from the revolt of
slaves led by Spartacus, the more so since two other
commanders (L. Gellius Publicola and Cn. Lentulus
Clodianus) had previously failed in that attempt. The
other consul, Pompey, could equally point to military
success in the 70s, against Sertorius in Spain, though
his election was perhaps still more spectacular, since
he was six years below the minimum age for election
as consul. The year 70 was also remarkable for legislation: by L. Aurelius Cotta to remove once more the
monopoly of jury membership which the senate had
held since the time of Sulla in 81; and by Pompey and
Crassus themselves, to restore to the *tribuni plebis*
the power to initiate legislation which also had been
removed at Sulla's instigation.

Indeed, a principal part of Sulla's programme
had been aimed at curtailing the power of *tribuni
plebis*, in the belief that their use of it since the time
of Tiberius Gracchus (133 B.C.) had militated against
good senatorial government. Pompey, in sponsoring
the legislation to restore that power, was acting in
response to agitation during the decade of the 70s,
and there seems to have been a widespread feeling
that this restoration was inevitable if the Sullan
system was to survive at all. Nevertheless, those who
believed that *tribuni plebis* would use their revived
power to undermine that system soon found confirm-
ation of their view. Of the *tribuni plebis* Cornelius
and Gabinius (67) and Manilius (66), the last two each
took advantage of their restored powers to promote
legislation which gave Pompey major new responsi-
bilities: in combating piracy (the *lex Gabinia*), and in
pursuing the war against Mithridates of Pontus (the
lex Manilia). Manilius' proposal was supported also by
Cicero, whose speech *de imperio Cn. Pompeii* (or *de*

lege Manilia) survives. The tactics of these *tribuni plebis* (like Cornelius - see below) were the familiar ones of proposing their bills directly to the *populus* without consulting the senate first, and attempting to vote from office other *tribuni plebis* who used their veto to obstruct them. In outlining Cornelius' previous career, Asconius points out that he had already served under Pompey, and was now meeting stiff opposition to his own proposals as *tribunus plebis* from "the senate" (i.e. the *optimates* - see Glossary p. 151). These proposals did in fact correspond very closely the issues to which Pompey had drawn attention during his candidature for the consulship (at a *contio* called by M. Lollius Palicanus) - the powers of *tribuni plebis*, justice in the government of provinces, protection of provincials.

It is noticeable that Cornelius enjoyed quite wide support for the substance of his proposals, especially those on the conduct of praetors and on dispensation from the law (see Exposition below, A. p. 93); it was his methods which aroused hostility (Asconius remarks that his "behaviour was seen as unreasonably tenacious"). When this opposition crystallized into a charge of *maiestas* in 65 B.C., Cicero unsurprisingly took on his defence, "no doubt in order to please Pompey" (E. Badian, *OCD*[2] s.v. Cornelius (1)). Clearly the persons who spoke against Cornelius saw the issue as being the power of the *tribuni plebis* (A. p. 121). The fact that the *tribunus plebis* P. Servilius Globulus supported Cornelius at the trial (A. p. 97), in contrast to his previous actions, points to the same conclusion.

Of the speech Cicero delivered, we possess only the passages which Asconius chooses to quote for comment. However there is an account of Cornelius in Cassius Dio (36.38) which diverges from Asconius in emphasis. Of the modern writers cited above, McDonald attempts to reconcile the two versions, while Griffin tends to prefer Asconius.

IV. PRO CORNELIO DE MAIESTATE

(57) Hanc orationem dixit L. Cotta L. Torquato coss. post annum quam superiores.

A R G V M E N T V M

C. Cornelius homo non improbus vita habitus est. Fuerat quaestor Cn. Pompeii, dein tribunus plebis C. Pisone M'. Glabrione coss. biennio ante quam haec dicta sunt.

In eo magistratu ita se gessit ut iusto pertinacior videretur. Alienatus autem a senatu est ex hac causa. Rettulerat ad senatum ut, quoniam exterarum nationum legatis pecunia magna daretur usura turpiaque et famosa ex eo lucra fierent, ne quis legatis exterarum nationum pecuniam expensam ferret. Cuius relationem repudiavit senatus et decrevit satis cautum videri eo S.C. quod aliquot ante annos L. Domitio C. Caelio coss. factum erat, cum senatus ante pauculos annos ex eodem illo S.C. decrevisset ne quis Cretensibus pecuniam mutuam daret. Cornelius ea re *(58)* offensus senatui questus est de ea in contione: exhauriri provincias usuris; providendum ut haberent legati unde praesenti die darent; promulgavitque legem qua auctoritatem senatus minuebat, ne quis nisi per populum legibus solveretur. Quod antiquo quoque iure erat cautum; itaque in omnibus S.C. quibus aliquem legibus solvi placebat adici erat solitum ut de ea re ad populum ferretur: sed paulatim ferri erat desitum resque iam in eam consuetudinem venerat ut postremo ne adiceretur quidem in senatus consultis de rogatione ad populum ferenda; eaque ipsa S.C. per pauculos admodum fiebant.

Indigne eam Corneli rogationem tulerant potentissimi quique ex senatu quorum gratia magnopere minuebatur; itaque P. Servilius Globulus tribunus plebis inventus erat qui C. Cornelio obsisteret. Is, ubi legis ferundae dies

IV. *Speech delivered on behalf of Cornelius on
a charge of* maiestas

(57) Cicero gave this speech in the consulship of L. Cotta
and L. Torquatus *(65 B.C.)*, a year after those included
above (≠).

EXPOSITION

C. Cornelius' career was thought fairly honourable. He
served as quaestor for Pompey, and then as *tribunus
plebis* during the consulship of C. Piso and M. Glabrio *(67
B.C.)*, two years before the present speech was given. His
behaviour in this office was seen as unreasonably tenacious, and he lost the support of the senate as a result.
He had proposed to the senate that since money was
being loaned to foreign delegations at interest, and
notorious and disreputable profits were being made, the
granting of funds to such delegations should be stopped.
The senate rejected this proposal, and held that adequate
steps had been taken in the decree passed some years
before in the consulship of L.(?) Domitius and C. Coelius[1]
(94 B.C.), since the senate, in accordance with that same
decree, had very recently forbidden the lending of money
to the Cretans. As he made no progress with the senate,
(58) Cornelius held a *contio* to protest. He maintained that
provinces were being exhausted by payment of interest,
and that steps should be taken to enable the delegates to
have the resources to pay on the appointed day. Then he
promoted a bill which diminished the senate's authority,
providing that only the *populus* could give dispensation
from the laws. (This stipulation was in fact contained in
an ancient law, and in any senatorial decree which
offered such a dispensation it was customary to add a
clause specifying that the *populus* was to be consulted
about it; however, this gradually ceased to be the
practice, and eventually the clause dealing with consul-
tation of the *populus* came to be omitted altogether from
senatorial decrees; and the decrees themselves were now
passed by a low turnout of members.)

The most powerful persons, whose influence was now
greatly threatened by Cornelius' proposal, expressed
outrage, and a *tribunus plebis* called P. Servilius Globulus
was found for the purpose of obstructing Cornelius. The

venit et praeco subiciente scriba verba legis recitare populo coepit, et scribam subicere et praeconem pronuntiare passus non est. Tum Cornelius ipse codicem recitavit.

Quod cum improbe fieri C. Piso consul vehementer quereretur tollique tribuniciam intercessionem diceret, gravi convicio a populo exceptus est; et cum ille eos qui sibi intentabant manus prendi a lictore iussisset, fracti eius fasces sunt lapidesque etiam ex ultima contione in consulem iacti: quo tumultu Cornelius perturbatus concilium dimisit actutum.

Actum deinde eadem de re in senatu est magnis contentionibus. Tum Cornelius *(59)* ita ferre rursus coepit ne quis in senatu legibus solveretur nisi CC adfuissent, neve quis, cum solutus esset, intercederet, cum de ea re ad populum ferretur. Haec sine tumultu res acta est. Nemo enim negare poterat pro senatus auctoritate esse eam legem; sed tamen eam tulit invitis optimatibus, qui per paucos amicis gratificari solebant.

Aliam deinde legem Cornelius, etsi nemo repugnare ausus est, multis tamen invitis tulit, ut praetores ex edictis suis perpetuis ius dicerent: quae res studium aut gratiam ambitiosis praetoribus qui varie ius dicere assueverant sustulit.

Alias quoque complures leges Cornelius promulgavit, quibus plerisque collegae intercesserunt: per quas contentiones totius tribunatus eius tempus peractum est.

Sequenti deinde anno M'. Lepido L. Volcacio coss., quo anno praetor Cicero fuit, reum Cornelium duo fratres Cominii lege Cornelia de maiestate fecerunt. Detulit nomen Publius, subscripsit Gaius.

Et cum P. Cassius praetor decimo die, ut mos est, adesse iussisset, eoque die ipse non adfuisset seu avocatus propter publici frumenti curam seu gratificans reo, circumventi sunt ante tribunal eius accusatores a notis operarum ducibus ita ut mors intentaretur, si mox non *(60)* desisterent.

Quam perniciem vix effugerunt interventu consulum

day arrived for the passage of the bill, and the herald began to declaim the text of the bill to the *populus*, with the clerk prompting him; Globulus then refused to allow the clerk to prompt or the herald to speak. Cornelius himself started reading the text. The consul C. Piso then protested vehemently that this was improper, and that the *tribunus plebis'* veto was being ignored. This was greeted with a huge uproar from the *populus*; Piso ordered those who were threatening him to be arrested by the lictor, but his rods of office were smashed and he was pelted with stones from the rear of the *contio*. Cornelius was much upset by the tumult and immediately closed the meeting. After this there was much fervent argument in the senate about the issue, *(59)* and Cornelius tried to bring forward a further motion that a dispensation from the law should be granted only if 200 members attended, and that no-one if so dispensed should record a veto when the matter was put to the *populus*. This was passed in an orderly session, since this measure indisputably favoured the senate's authority; but it gained the hostility of the *optimates* who used a small attendance to enable them to assist their friends.

Thereupon Cornelius moved another bill, which was widely criticized, even though no-one actually obstructed it: this stipulated that praetors should dispense justice strictly in accordance with their own edicts. The effect of the measure was to frustrate the quest for influence by ambitious praetors who had made a habit of dispensing justice inconsistently. There were other bills promoted by Cornelius also, most of them vetoed by his colleagues; in fact his entire term as *tribunus plebis* was one of stress and dissension.

The following year (the consulship of M'. Lepidus and Volcacius Tullus, and the praetorship of Cicero) *(66 B.C.)* Cornelius was prosecuted by the two brothers Cominius under the law of Cornelius Sulla on *maiestas*. Publius Cominius laid the charge, and his brother Gaius added his signature. The praetor P. Cassius ordered the defendant to appear ten days later, in the normal way; but on the day Cassius himself failed to appear (perhaps he was detained by business of the corn supply, or maybe he did it to help the defendant); at all events the prosecutors were surrounded in front of the dais by some notorious gang-leaders, and their lives were threatened if they did not drop the charges. *(60)* They narrowly escaped this

qui advocati reo descenderant. Et cum in scalas quasdam Cominii fugissent, clausi in noctem ibi se occultaverunt, deinde per tecta vicinarum aedium profugerunt ex urbe.

Postero die, cum P. Cassius adsedisset et citati accusatores non adessent, exemptum nomen est de reis Corneli; Cominii autem magna infamia flagraverunt vendidisse silentium magna pecunia.

Sequente deinde anno L. Cotta L. Torquato coss., quo haec oratio a Cicerone praetura nuper peracta dicta est, cum primum apparuisset Manilius qui iudicium per operarum duces turbaverat, deinde quod ex S.C. ambo consules . . . praesidebant ei iudicio, non respondisset atque esset damnatus, recreavit se Cominius, ut infamiam acceptae pecuniae tolleret, ac repetiit Cornelium lege maiestatis. Res acta est magna exspectatione. Paucos autem comites Cornelius perterritus Manili exitu . . . in iudicium adhibuit, ut ne clamor quidem ullus ab advocatis eius oriretur.

Dixerunt in eum infesti testimonia principes civitatis qui plurimum in senatu poterant Q. Hortensius, Q. Catulus, Q. Metellus Pius, M. Lucullus, M'. Lepidus. Dixerunt autem hoc: vidisse se cum Cornelius in tribunatu codicem *(61)* pro rostris ipse recitaret, quod ante Cornelium nemo fecisse existimaretur. Volebant videri se iudicare eam rem magnopere ad crimen imminutae maiestatis tribuniciae pertinere; etenim prope tollebatur intercessio, si id tribunis permitteretur.

Non poterat negare id factum esse Cicero, is eo confugit ut diceret non ideo quod lectus sit codex a tribuno imminutam esse tribuniciam potestatem. Qua vero arte et scientia orationis ita ut et dignitatem clarissimorum civium contra quos dicebat non violaret, et tamen auctoritate eorum laedi reum non pateretur, quantaque moderatione rem tam difficilem aliis tractaverit lectio ipsa declarabit.

Adiumentum autem habuit quod, sicut diximus, Cornelius praeter destrictum propositum animi adversus principum voluntatem cetera vita nihil fecerat quod magnopere improbaretur; praeterea quod et ipse Globulus

fate when the consuls, who had arrived to speak for the defendant, intervened. The Cominii ran away up some stairs, and went into hiding for the night; later they got away from the city over the neighbouring rooftops. Next day P. Cassius took his seat in court, the prosecutors failed to come, and Cornelius' name was removed from the list of defendants. Excited rumours flew around that the Cominii had sold their silence for a large sum.

The next year (the consulship of L. Cotta and L. Torquatus) *(65 B.C.)* was the one in which Cicero delivered this speech, shortly after he had completed his praetorship. The Manilius who had arranged the disruption of the court by gang-leaders made his appearance; and by a decree of the senate both consuls were in attendance at the trial. He made no reply to the charges and was convicted; thereupon Cominius revived his activities and again prosecuted Cornelius for *maiestas*, in order to dissipate the allegation of having taken bribes. There was great excitement at the hearing: however, Cornelius was frightened by Manilius' downfall, and brought only a few friends with him as sponsors; not the slightest sound came from his supporters.

Certain political leaders, who were influential in the senate and were his opponents, gave evidence: Q. Hortensius, Q. Catulus, Q. Metellus Pius, M. Lucullus, M'. Lepidus.[2] Their statement was that they had seen Cornelius as *tribunus plebis* reading out his text personally in front of the platform, *(61)* something that no-one had apparently ever done before. They wanted it to be seen to be their view that this action strongly supported a charge of damage to the *maiestas* of a tribune – if after all *tribuni plebis* were allowed to do this, the principle of the veto was rendered almost void. Cicero could not deny the facts, so he resorted to the argument that tribunician powers were not diminished by the reading out of the text by the *tribunus plebis*. A study of this speech will show the skill and understanding of oratory with which Cicero ensured both that he did not assault the standing of his distinguished opponents and that he did not let the defendant be undermined by their influence; it will also display the moderation of his handling of a task that others found so difficult.

Certainly he had one advantage: as we have said, Cornelius had done nothing in his career to attract

qui intercesserat aderat Cornelio, et – quod ipsum quoque diximus – quod Cornelius Pompeii Magni quaestor fuerat, apud duas decurias profuit equitum Romanorum et tribunorum aerariorum et ex tertia quoque parte senatorum apud plerosque exceptis eis qui erant familiares principum civitatis.

Res acta est magno conventu, magnaque exspectatione quis eventus iudicii futurus esset . . . a summis viris dici testimonia et id quod ei dicerent confiteri reum animadvertebant. Exstat oratio Comini accusatoris quam sumere in manus est aliquod *(62)* operae pretium, non solum propter Ciceronis orationes quas pro Cornelio habemus sed etiam propter semet ipsam.

Cicero, ut ipse significat, quatriduo Cornelium defendit; quas actiones contulisse eum in duas orationes apparet. Iudicium id exercuit Q. Gallius praetor.

[In hac causa tres sunt quaestiones: prima, cum sit Cornelius reus maiestatis legis Corneliae, utrum certae aliquae res sint ea lege comprehensae quibus solis reus maiestatis teneatur, quod patronus defendit; an libera eius interpretatio iudici relicta sit, quod accusator proponit. Secunda est an quod Cornelius fecit †ne ca maiestatis teneatur. Tertia an minuendae maiestatis animum habuerit.]

ENARRATIO

VER. A PRIMO CIRCI. CLX

Postulatur apud me praetorem primum de pecuniis repetundis. Prospectat videlicet Cominius quid agatur: videt homines faeneos in medium ad temptandum periculum proiectos.

Simulacra effigie hominum ex faeno fieri solebant quibus obiectis ad spectaculum praebendum tauri irritarentur.

Quid? Metellus summa nobilitate ac virtute, cum bis iurasset, semel privatim, iterum lege, privatim (63) patris, publice legis . . . deiectus est? ratione an vi? at utrimque

criticism, apart from showing a ruthless attitude towards the wishes of leading politicians; then there was the fact that the Globulus who had earlier used his veto was appearing on Cornelius' behalf; furthermore, as I have also explained, Cornelius had been quaestor to Pompey, which stood to his credit with two of the jury-panels (*equites* and *tribuni aerarii*), and with most of the third (senators) except for the relatives of these leading politicians.

The occasion attracted a huge attendance, and there was great excitement about the outcome: it was observed that some most distinguished men were offering evidence, and that the accused was expressing agreement with what they said. There is in existence the speech of Cominius the prosecutor,[3] and it is worth consulting it, *(62)* not just because we possess Cicero's speeches on Cornelius' behalf, but for its own sake also. Cicero took four days to defend Cornelius, as he makes clear himself; and he presented this defence in the form of two speeches.[4] The president of the court was the praetor Q. Gallius.

(In this case there are three issues: First, given that Cornelius is on trial for *maiestas* under the Cornelian law, are there certain acts covered by that law which alone sustain a charge of *maiestas* (as the defence counsel argues)? Or is a looser construction of the law necessary, as the prosecutor asserts? Second, there is the question whether what Cornelius did should count as *maiestas* (?); and third, did he have an intent to commit *maiestas*?)

COMMENTARY

(about 160 lines from the start)
He was brought before me as praetor the first time on a charge of repetundae: *no doubt Cominius was testing the prospects, and planting straw men in the open to help assess the threat.*

It used to be the practice to make imitation men out of straw, and then exhibit them to provoke the bull and so create entertainment.

Metellus, a man of the greatest distinction and courage, took the oath twice, (63) once in a personal capacity, and a second time by the law – privately in the name of his father, publicly in that of the law (?): was he then induced to desist? Was it by persuasion or by force?

*omnem suspicionem animi tollit et C. Curionis virtus ac
dignitas et Q. Metelli spectata adulescentia ad summam
laudem omnibus rebus ornata.*

Hoc exemplum affert hoc loco, quod vult probare
desistere eum debere ab accusatione - quamvis neque
accusatus sit neque fecerit pactionem - nam Metellus et
postulaverat Curionem et destiterat. Confugit autem orator
ad Metelli nobilitatem et ad C. Curionis industriam ut
tegeret id quod illi utilius quam honestius fecerant.

Res autem tota se sic habet: in qua quidem illud
primum explicandum est, de quo Metello hoc dicit. Fuerunt
enim tunc plures Quinti Metelli, ex quibus duo consulares,
Pius et Creticus, de quibus apparet eum non dicere, duo
autem adulescentes, Nepos et Celer, ex quibus nunc
Nepotem significat. Eius enim patrem Q. Metellum Nepotem,
Baliarici filium, Macedonici nepotem qui consul fuit cum T.
Didio, Curio is de quo loquitur accusavit: isque Metellus
moriens petiit ab hoc filio suo Metello ut Curionem
accusatorem suum accusaret, et id facturum esse iure
iurando adegit. Metellus fecit reum Curionem; cumque
interim quendam civem idem Metellus servum suum esse
contendens vi arripuisset ac verberibus affecisset, Curio
assertorem ei comparavit. Dein cum appareret eum exitum
iudicii illius futurum ut *(64)* liber is iudicaretur quem
Metellus verberibus affectum esse negare non poterat,
inter Metellum et Curionem facta concordia est pactione ut
neque arbitrium de libertate perageretur, esset tamen ille
in libertate de quo agebatur, neque Metellus perstaret in
accusatione Curionis: eaque pactio ab utroque servata est.

Huc ergo illud pertinet, cum iurasse dixit semel
privatim . . . iterum lege, tum scilicet cum in Curionem
calumniam iuravit. Cum hoc autem Metello postea Cicero
simultates gessit; evasit enim Metellus malus atque
improbus civis.

Legem, inquit, de libertinorum suffragiis Cornelius C.
Manilio dedit. Quid est hoc *dedit*? Attulit? an rogavit? an
hortatus est? Attulisse ridiculum est, quasi legem aliquam
aut ad scribendum difficilem aut ad excogitandum recon-
ditam: quae lex paucis his annis non modo scripta sed
etiam lata esset.

Surely any suspicion is removed by the courage and distinction of C. Curio and the youthful career of Q. Metellus which has been shown to be so entirely admirable.

He adduces such an instance at this point because he wants to demonstrate that the man should give up his prosecution (though he himself had not been prosecuted nor had concluded any deal) – Metellus had after all charged Curio and then withdrawn. The orator makes much of Metellus' distinction and C. Curio's efforts so as to conceal the fact that what they had done was advantageous rather than honourable. The story in fact goes as follows: – though first I must explain which Metellus he is referring to. There were several men called Quintus Metellus at the time; two were ex-consuls – Pius and Creticus – and he does not mean them; there were also two young members of the family, Nepos and Celer, and it is Nepos he is talking about. This man's father Q. Metellus Nepos, son of Baliaricus, and grandson of the Macedonicus who was consul with T. Didius (*98 B.C.*), was prosecuted by the Curio mentioned already. At his death Metellus requested this Metellus, his son, to prosecute his accuser Curio, and made him take an oath to do so. Metellus then charged Curio. Meanwhile Metellus seized and assaulted a man who was a citizen, claiming that he was a slave, and Curio secured the man's help in his defence. It soon became clear that the case would result in this man's being adjudged a free man *(64)* (and Metellus could not deny having committed the assault), and so a congenial agreement was made that the question of this man's status would not be taken any further, but that he would be treated as free: in return Metellus would not persist with the prosecution of Curio; both men kept their bargain. The point of saying then that he took the oath once in a personal capacity and a second time by the law is that his oath in Curio's case was an instance of bad faith. Cicero later on came into conflict with this Metellus, who turned out an evil and dishonourable citizen.

He says that Cornelius gave out to C. Manilius the law on the franchise of sons of freedmen. "Gave out"? Does this mean "brought forth", "proposed", "supported"? To mean "brought forth" seems silly, as if it were a law difficult to write or requiring great intellectual effort: in fact this law was both set down and passed during these

P. Sulpicium in tribunatu hanc eandem legem tulisse iam significavimus. Tulit autem L. Sulla qui postea Felix appellatus est Q. Pompeio consulibus ante XXIII annos quam haec dicta sunt, cum per vim rem p. possedisset et ab initiis bonarum actionum ad perditas progressus esset: quod et initium bellorum civilium fuit, et propter quod ipse Sulpicius consulum armis iure oppressus esse visus est.

(65) In quo cum multa reprehensa sint, tum imprimis celeritas actionis.

Celeritatem actionis significat, quod Manilius, sicut iam ostendimus, post pauculos statim dies quam inierat tribunatum legem eandem Compitalibus pertulit.

Petivit tamen a me praetor maxima contentione ut causam Manili defenderem.

C. Attium Celsum significat, sicut iam ante dictum est.

VER. A PRI. DCCCL

Dicit de eodem Manili tribunatu:
Nam cum is tr.pl. duas leges in eo magistratu tulisset, unam perniciosam, alteram egregiam: quod summae rei p. nocuisset ab illo ipso tr. abiectum est, bonum autem quod . . . summa resp. manet et †in vestri ordina . . . dis fuit.

Dictum est iam supra de his legibus, quarum una de libertinorum suffragiis, quae cum S.C. damnata esset, ab ipso quoque Manilio non ultra defensa est: altera de bello Mithridatico Cn. Pompeio extra ordinem mandando, ex qua lege tum Magnus Pompeius bellum gerebat.

(66) Dicit de disturbato iudicio Maniliano:
Aliis ille in illum furorem magnis hominibus auctoribus impulsus est qui aliquod institui exemplum disturbandorum iudiciorum reip. perniciosissimum, temporibus suis accommodatissimum, meis alienissimum rationibus cupiverunt.

L. Catilinam et Cn. Pisonem videtur significare. Fuit autem Catilina patricius et eodem illo tempore erat reus repetundarum, cum provinciam Africam obtinuisset et consulatus candidatum se ostendisset. Accusator erat eius

few years.

We have already mentioned (≠) that P. Sulpicius had passed this same law during his term as *tribunus plebis*; this was in the consulship of L. Sulla (later titled *Felix*) and Q. Pompeius (*88 B.C.*), 23 years before the present speech. Sulpicius had seized control by force, and began well but deteriorated into contemptible behaviour; this was the prelude to civil war, and as a result the defeat of Sulpicius by consular armies was regarded as just.

(65) Many criticisms were made of this, especially that of undue haste.

The "undue haste" consists in the fact that Manilius, as previously mentioned (≠), passed this same law at the time of the Compitalia a few days after entering office as *tribunus plebis*.

The praetor requested me with the utmost earnestness to undertake the defence of Manilius.

He means C. Attius Celsus, as I said earlier (≠).

(850 lines from the start)
He also says this about Manilius' term as *tribunus plebis*:

This tribunus plebis *passed two laws in that office, one being vicious and the other admirable: the harm that might have been done to the state was prevented by this very man, while the benefit which the common good demanded has survived and . . . (?)*

I have already mentioned these laws (≠): one concerned the franchise of sons of freedmen; disapproval of it was expressed by a decree of the senate, and Manilius did not persist in promoting it. The other law concerned the granting to Pompey of an extraordinary command over the war against Mithridates: Pompey was at this time fighting the war under this law. *(66)* Cicero further remarks about the upheavals at Manilius' trial:

He was driven to this violent behaviour at the instigation of other powerful men: they wanted to create a significant disruption of the courts which was highly damaging to the state, while being well suited to their purposes, but entirely out of keeping with my methods.

He appears to mean L. Catilina and Cn. Piso. Catilina, a *patricius*, was on trial at that time for *repetundae*, having governed the province of Africa and declared his candidature for the consulship.[5] He was prosecuted by P.

P. Clodius, adulescens ipse quoque perditus, qui postea cum Cicerone inimicitias gessit. Cn. quoque Piso, adulescens potens et turbulentus, familiaris erat Catilinae omniumque consiliorumque eius particeps et turbarum auctor.

VER. CIR. cɔX

Possum dicere hominem summa prudentia spectatum, C. Cottam, de suis legibus abrogandis ipsum ad senatum rettulisse.

Hic est Cotta de quo iam saepe diximus, magnus orator habitus et compar in ea gloria P. Sulpicio et C. Caesari . . . Videntur autem in rebus parvis fuisse leges illae, quas cum tulisset, rettulit de eis abrogandis ad senatum. Nam neque apud Sallustium neque apud Livium neque apud Fenestellam ullius alterius latae ab eo legis est mentio *(67)* praeter eam quam in consulatu tulit invita nobilitate magno populi studio, ut eis qui tr.pl. fuissent alios quoque magistratus capere liceret; quod lex a dictatore L. Sulla paucis ante annis lata prohibebat: neque eam Cottae legem abrogatam esse significat.

SEQVITVR

Possum etiam eiusdem Cottae legem de iudiciis privatis anno post quam lata sit a fratre eius abrogatam.

M. Cottam significat. Fuerunt autem fratres tres: duo hi, C., M., tertius L. Cotta qui lege sua iudicia inter tres ordines communicavit senatum, equites, tribunos aerarios; adeptique sunt omnes consulatum.

STATIM

Legem Liciniam et Muciam de civibus redigendis video constare inter omnis, quamquam duo consules omnium quos vidimus sapientissimi tulissent, non modo inutilem sed perniciosam rei publicae fuisse.

L. Licinium Crassum oratorem et Q. Mucium Scaevolam pont. max. eundemque et oratorem et iuris consultum significat. Hi enim legem eam de qua loquitur de redigendis in suas civitates sociis in consulatu tulerunt. Nam

Clodius, himself a vicious young man, who later on pursued a feud with Cicero. Cn. Piso too was an influential and violent young man, who was related to Catilina and was an accomplice in his activities and a promoter of disturbances.

(about line 1010)
I might point out that C. Cotta, a man well known for good judgment, made a proposal to the senate to repeal his own laws.

I have mentioned this Cotta often before (≠): he was regarded as a powerful orator, the equal of P. Sulpicius and C. Caesar. (. . .) When he had passed these laws, which were apparently concerned with trivial matters, he proposed to the senate that they should be repealed. There is no mention of another law passed by him in Sallustius, Livius, or Fenestella, *(67)* apart from the one passed during his consulship (*75 B.C.*) amid much enthusiasm from the *populus* and disapproval by the *nobiles*; this provided that those who had been *tribuni plebis* should be allowed to hold further office, a step forbidden by L. Sulla's law passed a few years previously. Cicero does not mean that it was this law of Cotta that was repealed.

(next comes the following)
I might further mention that this same Cotta's law on private suits was repealed in the year after its passage by his brother.

It is M. Cotta who is meant. There were three brothers altogether: these two, C. and M., and thirdly L. Cotta, who legislated to share membership of juries between senators, *equites*, and *tribuni aerarii*; all three reached the consulship.

(immediately afterwards)
As for the lex Licinia Mucia *concerning the withdrawal of the rights of citizenship, all are agreed, I observe, that it was passed by two consuls who were the most judicious we have known, and yet that to the state it was not merely unhelpful but actually destructive.*

He is referring to the orator L. Licinius Crassus and to Q. Mucius Scaevola, who was chief priest, orator, and jurist. During their consulship (*95 B.C.*) they passed the law Cicero is speaking of, which provided that Italians

cum *(68)* summa cupiditate civitatis Romanae Italici populi tenerentur et ob id magna pars eorum pro civibus Romanis se gereret, necessaria lex visa est ut in suae quisque civitatis ius redigeretur. Verum ea lege ita alienati animi sunt principum Italicorum populorum ut ea vel maxima causa belli Italici quod post triennium exortum est fuerit.

Quattuor omnino genera sunt, iudices, in quibus per senatum more maiorum statuatur aliquid de legibus. Vnum est eius modi placere legem abrogari: ut Q. Caecilio M. Iunio coss. quae leges rem militarem impedirent, ut abrogarentur.

Q. Caecilius Metellus Numidicus, M. Iunius Silanus, de quibus facit mentionem, consules fuerunt bello Cimbrico quod diu prave simul et infeliciter administratum est; atque ipse quoque hic Iunius male rem adversus Cimbros gessit . . . †ac plures leges quae per eos annos †quibus hec significabantur populo latae erant, quibus militiae stipendia minuebantur, abrogavit.

Alterum, quae lex lata esse dicatur, ea non videri populum teneri: ut L. Marcio Sex. Iulio coss. de legibus Liviis.

Puto vos reminisci has esse leges Livias quas illis consulibus *(69)* M. Livius Drusus tribunus plebis tulerit. Qui cum senatus partes tuendas suscepisset et leges pro optimatibus tulisset, postea eo licentiae est progressus ut nullum in his morem servaret. Itaque Philippus cos. qui ei inimicus erat obtinuit a senatu ut leges eius omnes uno S.C. tollerentur. Decretum est enim contra auspicia esse latas neque eis teneri populum.

Tertium est de legum derogationibus –: quo de genere persaepe S.C. fiunt, ut nuper de ipsa lege Calpurnia cui derogaretur.

Lex haec Calpurnia de ambitu erat. Tulerat eam ante biennium C. Calpurnius Piso cos., in qua praeter alias poenas pecuniaria quoque poena erat adiecta.

should be restored to their own *civitates*. *(68)* The peoples of Italy desired Roman citizenship most earnestly, and a large number of them were passing themselves off as Roman citizens; hence it was felt necessary to legislate to restore them to the jurisdiction of their own *civitates*. However, this created such discontent among the leaders of the peoples of Italy that it constituted perhaps the most important reason for the Italian War which broke out three years later.

Gentlemen, there are generally four ways in which a decision about the law can be traditionally taken by the senate: one of these is a proposal to repeal a law, as was done during the consulship of Q. Caecilius and M. Iunius in the case of laws which obstructed the military effort.

He is referring to Q. Caecilius Metellus Numidicus and M. Iunius Silanus, who were consuls (*109 B.C.*) at the time of the war against the Cimbri, a war being conducted inefficiently and unproductively; indeed Iunius himself had little success against this enemy. So he repealed a number of laws passed during this time by the *populus*, which had the effect of reducing the rewards of military service.

The second way is to reach agreement that although a law has allegedly been passed, the populus is not bound by it, as in the case of the Livian laws during the consulship of L. Marcius and Sex. Iulius.

You no doubt recall (≠) that these were the Livian laws passed during these men's consulship *(69)* by the *tribunus plebis* M. Livius Drusus (*91 B.C.*). This man had undertaken to safeguard the senate's interests and had legislated in favour of the *optimates*; whereupon he abandoned all restraint in his behaviour. Therefore his opponent, the consul Philippus, obtained leave to have all his legislation repealed by a single decree of the senate, on the grounds that it had been passed in defiance of the auspices and that the *populus* was not bound by it.

The third method is partial abrogation, which is often the subject of senatorial decrees, as in the recent case of the law of Calpurnius.

This is Calpurnius' law concerning bribery, passed two years earlier by the consul C. Calpurnius Piso (*67 B.C.*); besides other penalties it prescribed in addition a

P. Africanus ille superior, ut dicitur, non solum a sapientissimis hominibus qui tum erant verum etiam a se ipso saepe accusatus est quod, cum consul esset cum Ti. Longo, passus esset tum primum a populari consessu senatoria subsellia separari.

Hoc factum est secundo consulatu Scipionis post septimum annum quam Carthaginiensibus bello secundo data est pax.

Factum id esse autem Antias tradidit ludis Romanis quos fecerunt aediles curules C. Atilius Serranus, L. Scribonius Libo, et id eos fecisse iussu censorum Sex. Aeli Paeti, C. Corneli Cethegi. Et videtur in hac quidem oratione hunc auctorem secutus Cicero dixisse passum esse *(70)* Scipionem secerni a cetero consessu spectacula senatorum. In ea autem quam post aliquot annos habuit de haruspicum responso, non passum esse Scipionem, sed ipsum auctorem fuisse dandi eum locum senatoribus videtur significare.

Verba eius haec sunt:

Nam quid ego de illis ludis loquar quos in Palatio nostri maiores ante templum Matris Magnae fieri celebrarique voluerunt? - quibus primum ludis ante populi consessum senatui locum P. Africanus II cos. ille maior dedit . . .

Et collega eius Sempronio Longo hoc tributum esse senatui scribit, sed sine mentione Megalesium - aediles enim eos ludos facere soliti erant - votivis ludis factum tradit quos Scipio et Longus coss. fecerint.

Non praeterire autem vos volo esse oratoriae calliditatis ius ut, cum opus est, eisdem rebus ab utraque parte vel a contrariis utantur. Nam cum secundum Ciceronis opinionem auctore Scipione consule aediles secretum ante omnis locum spectandi senatoribus dederint, de eodem illo facto Scipionis in hac quidem oratione, quia causa popularis erat premebaturque senatus auctoritate atque ob id dignitatem eius ordinis quam posset maxime elevari causae expediebat, paenituisse ait Scipionem quod passus esset id fieri; in ea vero de haruspicum responso, quia in senatu habebatur cuius artibus erat blandiendum,

financial one.

We are told that P. Africanus the Elder was charged by the most judicious men of the day - and indeed he frequently blamed himself for it - with having permitted the senate's seats to be set apart for the first time from the rest during his consulship with Ti. Longus.

This occurred during Scipio's second consulship (*194 B.C.*), seven years after peace brought an end to the Second Punic War. Now Antias has recorded that it was done at the Roman Games presented by the curule *aediles* C. Atilius Serranus and L. Scribonius Libo, and that the *censores* Sex. Aelius Paetus and C. Cornelius Cethegus gave the instructions for this step. Certainly in this present speech Cicero seems to follow Antias in saying *(70)* that Scipio *permitted* the senators' accommodation to be separated from the rest. But in the speech "On the response of the soothsayers", delivered a few years later (*56 B.C.*), he seems to indicate that Scipio did not permit this privilege to be given to the senate but rather initiated the move himself. The text reads as follows:

What shall I say of the games which our forbears wished to be ritually celebrated on the Palatine before the temple of the Great Mother? At these games for the first time P. Africanus the Elder, in his second consulship, granted to the senate permission to be seated before the *populus* took their seats. . .[6]

And . . . [Fenestella?] writes that this privilege was conferred on the senate by Scipio and (?) his colleague Sempronius Longus;[7] though he does not mention the Megalensian Games - these being normally presented by *aediles* - and tells us that it was done at the votive games presented by Scipio and Longus as consuls (*194 B.C.*).

Now I should not like you to fail to notice this instance of an orator's skill in using the same material, when necessary, to argue opposing or even incompatible positions. Thus: it is Cicero's belief that the *aediles*, at Scipio's suggestion, granted the senate the privilege of being seated separately at the games before everyone else; in this speech, because the case was one with a popular appeal, while at the same time the senate's influence was oppressive, Cicero found it advantageous to

et magnopere illum laudat et non auctorem fuisse dandi – nam id erat levius – sed ipsum etiam dedisse dicit.

(71) CIRCA MEDIVM

Quo loco enumerat, cum lex feratur, quot loca intercessionis sint, ante quam qui legem fert populum iubeat discedere.

Est utique ius vetandi, cum ea feratur, quam diu . . . ferundi transferuntur; id est . . . lex, dum privati dicunt, dum . . . dum sitella defertur, dum aequantur sortes, dum sortitio fit, et si qua sunt alia huius generis.
†Alia populus confusus ut semper alias, ita et in contione. †Id peractis, cum id solum superest ut populus sententiam ferat, iubet eum is qui fert legem *discedere*: quod verbum non hoc significat quod in communi consuetudine est, eant de eo loco ubi lex feratur, sed in suam quisque tribum discedat in qua est suffragium laturus.

PAVLO POST

Vnum tamen quod hoc ipso tr.pl. factum est praetermittendum non videtur. Neque enim maius est legere codicem, cum intercedatur, quam sitellam ipsum coram ipso intercessore deferre, nec gravius incipere ferre quam perferre, nec vehementius ostendere se laturum invito collega quam ipsi collegae magistratum abrogare, nec criminosius tribus ad legem accipiendam quam ad collegam (72) reddendum privatum intro vocare: quae vir fortis, huius collega, A. Gabinius in re optima fecit omnia; neque cum salutem populo Romano atque omnibus gentibus finem diuturnae turpitudinis et servitutis afferret, passus est plus unius collegae sui quam universae civitatis vocem valere et voluntatem.

Manifestum est de ea lege Gabini Ciceronem nunc

the case to extol to the limit the prestige of that body; so
he says that Scipio regretted having permitted the move
to be made. But the speech "On the response of the
soothsayers" was delivered before the senate, whose
favour needed to be wooed; therefore Cicero applauds him
this time, and says not that he initiated the move (this
would not have been strong enough), but that he granted
the privilege himself.

(71) (about half way)
   At this point he identifies the opportunities for
placing a veto during the passage of a law, before the
stage when the legislating official closes the *populus'*
assembly:
   *The power of veto is available during a law's passage
while . . . are transferred; that is . . . while the law is
being read (?), while private citizens are speaking . . .
while the voting-urn is being produced, while the
allotment-tokens are being checked, while the voting is
actually in progress, and so forth.*
   Before this stage, the *populus,* when listening at a
contio, are an unorganized crowd as they always are
elsewhere. Now when the rest of the business is completed, the legislator bids them "disperse"; this word does
not carry its usual connotation, that they should leave
the place of the meeting; rather that they should divide
into their own tribal units in order to vote.

(shortly afterwards)
   But there is one incident while he was tribunus
plebis *that seems to deserve note: it is after all just as
serious to produce personally the voting-urn in the
presence of a man who is placing the veto as to persist
with reading a bill in defiance of the veto; it is just as
grave a matter to carry a bill as to set about proposing
it; it is just as violent to terminate a colleague's office as
to announce the intention of persevering with legislation
against his wishes; it is just as blameworthy to call upon
the tribal gatherings to strip a colleague of his magistracy* (72) *as to bid them give assent to a law. My client's
colleague, A. Gabinius, a courageous man, did indeed take
all these fine actions; and in bringing deliverance to the
Roman* populus *and an end to constant and despicable
servitude to all the nations, he did not permit the
expressed wish of a single colleague to overrule that of*

dicere qua Cn. Pompeio bellum adversus piratas datum est.

L. autem Trebellius est tribunus plebis quem non nominat: quo perseverante intercedere – nam senatui promiserat moriturum se ante quam illa lex perferretur – intro vocare tribus Gabinius coepit ut Trebellio magistratum abrogaret, sicut quondam Ti. Gracchus tribunus M. Octavio collegae suo magistratum abrogavit.

Et aliquam diu Trebellius ea re non perterritus aderat perstabatque in intercessione, quod id minari magis quam perseveraturum esse Gabinium arbitrabatur; sed post quam X et VII tribus rogationem acceperunt, ut una minus esset, et modo una supererat ut populi iussum conficeret, remisit intercessionem Trebellius: atque ita legem Gabinius de piratis persequendis pertulit.

At enim de corrigenda lege rettulerunt.
Diximus iam in principio Cornelium primo legem promulgasse ne quis per senatum lege solveretur, tum tulisse ut tum denique de ea re S.C. fieret, cum adessent in senatu non minus CC. Haec est illa quam appellat correctio.

(73) Idem, nisi haec ipsa lex quam C. Cornelius tulit obstitisset, decrevissent id quod palam iam isti defensores iudiciorum propugnaverunt, senatui non placere id iudicium de Sullae bonis fieri. Quam ego causam longe aliter praetor in contione defendi, cum id dicerem quod idem iudices postea statuerunt, iudicum aequiore tempore fieri oportere.
Quia defuerat superioribus temporibus in aerario pecunia publica, multa et saepe eius rei remedia erant quaesita; in quibus hoc quoque ut pecuniae publicae quae residuae apud quemque essent exigerentur.

Id autem maxime pertinebat ad Cornelium Faustum dictatoris filium, quia Sulla per multos annos quibus exercitibus praefuerat et rem publicam tenuerat sumpserat pecunias ex vectigalibus et ex aerario populi Romani; eaque res saepe erat agitata, saepe omissa partim propter gratiam Sullanarum partium, partim . . . quod iniquum

the entire country.

Clearly Cicero is now speaking of that law of Gabinius which entrusted the war against the pirates to Pompey. The unnamed *tribunus plebis* is L. Trebellius. This man had assured the senate that he would die rather than allow that law to be passed; so as he persisted in placing his veto, Gabinius began calling upon the tribes to vote on the removal of Trebellius from office, just as Ti. Gracchus had once done to his colleague M. Octavius (*133 B.C.*). For a while Trebellius was not deterred and continued his obstruction, thinking that Gabinius was expressing threats rather than a serious intent; however, 17 tribes supported the proposal, one less than was needed to constitute the will of the *populus*, so Trebellius then abandoned his veto; Gabinius thus secured the passage of his law concerning the campaign against the pirates.

Now they made a proposal to amend the law.

We said at the outset that Cornelius began by publishing a bill forbidding anyone to be exempted from the law by permission of the senate, and then a further one allowing that a decree of the senate could be passed on such an issue, provided that not less than 200 members were present. This is how the "amendment" arose.

(73) But for the obstacle presented by C. Cornelius' law, these same persons would have taken the decision which those defenders of the courts have already openly advocated, namely that the senate did not accept the judgment on the property of Sulla. I myself spoke in defence of this view at a contio *from a very different standpoint, when I was praetor; I argued as the jury later decided - that the decision should be taken at a more appropriate time.*

At an earlier period there had been a shortage of money in the public treasury, and many attempts had been made to find a solution: for example, by enacting that any public funds in private hands should be recovered. One man particularly concerned in this was Cornelius Faustus, son of the *dictator*; during his many years at the head of armies and of politics, his father Sulla had abstracted money from the tax-revenues and from the public treasury. The issue was frequently considered and then dropped, partly because of the

videbatur post tot annos ut quam quis pecuniam acceperat resque . . . redderet rationem.

STATIM

Antea vero quam multarum rerum iudicia sublata sint, et quia scitis praetereo et ne quem in iudicium oratio mea revocare videatur.

Bello Italico quod fuit adulescentibus illis qui tum in re publica vigebant, cum multi Varia lege inique damnarentur, quasi id bellum illis auctoribus conflatum esset, crebraeque *(74)* defectiones Italicorum nuntiarentur, nanctus iustitii occasionem senatus decrevit ne iudicia, dum tumultus Italicus esset, exercerentur: quod decretum eorum in contionibus populi saepe agitatum erat. Supererat autem ex eis qui illa iudicia metuerant vigens tum maxime C. Curio, pater Curionis adulescentis eius qui bello civili Caesaris fuit partium.

PAVLO POST

Non Cn. Dolabella C. Volcacium, honestissimum virum, communi et cotidiano iure privasset.

Duo fuerunt eo tempore Cn. Dolabellae, quorum alterum C. Caesar accusavit, alterum M. Scaurus.

Non denique homo illorum et vita et prudentia longe dissimilis, sed tamen nimis in gratificando iure liber, L. Sisenna, bonorum Cn. Corneli possessionem ex edicto suo P. Scipioni, adulescenti summa nobilitate, eximia virtute praedito, non dedisset.

Hoc solum hic adnotandum est hunc esse L. Sisennam qui res Romanas scripsit.

Qua re cum haec populus Romanus videret et cum a tribunis plebis docerentur, nisi poena accessisset in divisores, exstingui ambitum nullo modo posse, legem hanc Corneli flagitabat, illam quae ex (75) S.C. ferebatur repudiabat, idque iure, ut docti sumus duorum consulum designatorum calamitate –

influence of Sulla's group, partly because it seemed unfair that money acquired by anyone should after so many years . . . be the subject of proceedings for recovery.

(immediately afterwards)
A number of cases earlier on failed to come to court; because you are aware of this, I forbear to mention them, and I should not wish my present speech to cause proceedings in any case to restart.

The Italian War took place when men prominent in politics at the time of this speech were young. Under the law of Varius (*90 B.C.*) a number were wrongly convicted on the grounds that they had actually provoked the war; *(74)* and since revolts among the Italians were being frequently reported, the senate seized the opportunity provided by a period of public holiday to enact that legal cases should be suspended while the Italian emergency lasted. This decree brought much controversy at *contiones* of the *populus.* Of those who had lived in fear of these legal proceedings the most prominent now was C. Curio, father of the young Curio who supported Caesar in the Civil War.

(shortly afterwards)
Cn. Dolabella would not have deprived that honourable man C. Volcacius of the enduring rights that we all share.

At this time there were two Dolabellas, one prosecuted by C. Caesar, the other by M. Scaurus.
L. Sisenna, a man utterly unlike them in his way of life and intellect, but somewhat too ready to concede privileges – such a man I say would not have granted to that most nobilis and outstandingly courageous young man P. Scipio the possession of Cn. Cornelius' property by his own edict.

Here I must simply point out that this is the L. Sisenna who wrote a history of Rome.

The Roman populus realized, and was informed by the tribuni plebis, that without the imposition of penalties on the agents it was impossible to stamp out bribery; therefore it clamoured for Cornelius' law (75) and eschewed the one proposed in accordance with the decree of the senate – and rightly so, given the downfall of two consuls-elect which we have witnessed . . .

et eadem de re paulo post:

Vt spectaculum illud re et tempore salubre ac neces-
sarium, genere et exemplo miserum ac funestum videremus.
P. Sullam et P. Autronium significat, quorum alterum
L. Cotta, alterum L. Torquatus, qui cum haec Cicero
dicebat coss. erant, ambitus damnarant et in eorum locum
creati erant.

Quid ego nunc tibi argumentis respondeam posse fieri
ut alius aliquis Cornelius sit qui habeat Philerotem
servum; volgare nomen esse Philerotis, Cornelios vero ita
multos ut iam etiam collegium constitutum sit?
Frequenter tum etiam coetus factiosorum hominum sine
publica auctoritate malo publico fiebant: propter quod
postea collegia et S.C. et pluribus legibus sunt sublata
praeter pauca atque certa quae utilitas civitatis
desiderasset, sicut fabrorum fictorumque.

At enim extremi ac difficillimi temporis vocem illam, C.
Corneli, consulem mittere coegisti: qui rem p. salvam esse
vellent, ut ad legem accipiendam adessent.
C. Piso qui consul eodem anno fuit quo Cornelius
tribunus plebis erat, cum legem de ambitu ex S.C.
graviorem quam fuerat antea ferret et propter multitudinem divisorum qui per vim adversabantur e foro
eiectus esset, edixerat id *(76)* quod Cicero significat, et
maiore manu stipatus ad legem perferendam descenderat.

Plebem ex Maniliana offensione victam et domitam esse
dicit:
Aiunt vestros animos propter illius tribuni plebis
temeritatem posse adduci ut omnino nomine illius potes-
tatis abalienentur; qui restituerunt eam potestatem,
alterum nihil unum posse contra multos, alterum longe
abesse?
Manifestum puto esse vobis M. Crassum et Cn.
Pompeium significari, e quibus Crassus iudex tum sedebat
in Cornelium, Pompeius in Asia bellum Mithridaticum
gerebat.

Shortly afterwards comes a passage on the same topic:

And so we beheld that spectacle which was a salutary lesson in the circumstances, though deplorable in the precedent it set.

He is referring to P. Sulla and P. Autronius; the first was successfully prosecuted for bribery by L. Cotta, the second by L. Torquatus, and these two were appointed consuls in their place, an office held by them when Cicero delivered this speech.

How am I now to reply to you? Is it possible that there is some other Cornelius who owns a slave called Phileros? Is the name Phileros a common one - are there so many Corneliuses that they almost make up an assembly on their own?

Meetings frequently took place at the time, attended by disorderly men without proper sanction with damaging consequences. As a result the *collegia* were abolished by decrees of the senate and a number of laws later on, except for a few specified ones with a clear public benefit, such as those of carpenters and potters.

Now you, C. Cornelius, induced a consul to announce a most tense and difficult emergency, and to call upon those who valued their country's welfare to present themselves for the passage of the law, as he put it.

C. Piso was consul in the same year as Cornelius was *tribunus plebis.* He proposed a bill on the question of bribery, arising out of a decree of the senate, in stricter terms than the existing one. However, he was confronted by a violent demonstration by agents of bribery and forced out of the forum; *(76)* he then made the pronouncement to which Cicero refers, and returned to complete the passage of the bill, accompanied by a larger body of supporters.

As a result of the Manilius crisis he says that the *plebs* have been overwhelmed and reduced to subservience:

They say that because of the recklessness of that tribunus plebis you can be induced to surrender all claim to that power; that of those who restored that power the one can do nothing individually against so many, while the other is now far away.

It is clear, I imagine, that the reference is to M.

Tanta igitur in illis virtus fuit ut anno XVI post reges exactos propter nimiam dominationem potentium secederent, leges sacratas ipsi sibi restituerent, duo tribunos crearent, montem illum trans Anienem qui hodie Mons Sacer nominatus, in quo armati consederant, aeternae memoriae causa consecrarent. Itaque auspicato postero anno tr.pl. comitiis curiatis creati sunt.

Inducor magis librariorum hoc loco esse mendam quam ut Ciceronem parum proprio verbo usum esse credam.

Illo enim tempore de quo loquitur, quod fuit post XVI annos quam reges exacti sunt, plebs sibi leges sacratas non *restituit* – numquam enim tribunos plebis habuerat – sed tum primum eas *constituit.* Numerum quidem annorum post reges exactos cum id factum est diligenter posuit, isque fuit A. Verginio Tricosto L. Veturio Cicurino coss. Ceterum *(77)* quidam non duo tr.pl., ut Cicero dicit, sed quinque tradunt creatos tum esse singulos ex singulis classibus.

Sunt tamen qui eundem illum duorum numerum quem Cicero ponant: inter quos Tuditanus et Pomponius Atticus, Livius quoque noster. Idem hic et Tuditanus adiciunt tres praeterea ab illis duobus qui collegae essent lege creatos esse. Nomina duorum qui primi creati sunt haec traduntur: L. Sicinius L. f. Velutus, L. Albinius C. f. Paterculus.

Reliqua pars huius loci quae pertinet ad secundam constitutionem tribunorum et decemvirorum finitum imperium et breviter et aperte ab ipso dicitur. Nomina sola non adicit quis ille ex decemviris fuerit qui contra libertatem vindicias dederit, et quis ille pater contra cuius filiam id decrevit; scilicet quod notissimum est decemvirum illum Appium Claudium fuisse, patrem autem virginis L. Verginium. Vnum hoc tantum modo explicandum, quo loco primum de secunda secessione plebis, dehinc concordia facta, sic dicit:

Tum interposita fide per tris legatos amplissimos viros Romam armati revertuntur. In Aventino consederunt; inde armati in Capitolium venerunt; decem tr.pl. per pontificem, quod magistratus nullus erat, creaverunt.

Crassus and Pompey; Crassus at the time was sitting on the jury trying Cornelius, while Pompey was in Asia conducting the war against Mithridates.

Those men possessed such courage that in the sixteenth year after the expulsion of the kings they withdrew in the face of oppression by the powerful: they then restored their own sacred laws, appointed two tribuni, and consecrated as an everlasting shrine that hill across the Anio which today is called "mons sacer", where they had set up their armed encampment. Then in the following year with due ceremony tribuni plebis were appointed at the comitia curiata.

I incline to think that there is a scholar's error here, rather than that Cicero has used an unsuitable word. At the time he is speaking of, sixteen years after the expulsion of the kings, the *plebs* did not *restore* their sacred laws (they had never yet had *tribuni plebis*); they *instituted* them for the first time then. Cicero has carefully identified the number of years after the kings' expulsion that this event occurred - it being in the consulship of A. Verginius Tricostus and L. Veturius Cicurinus (*494 B.C.*). (*77*) However, some authorities speak of the appointment not of two but of five *tribuni plebis*, one from each of the classes of society. Some certainly do specify two as Cicero does: e.g. Tuditanus, Pomponius Atticus, and my compatriot Livius;[8] Tuditanus in fact says that three additional ones were appointed as colleagues by the existing two. The names of the first to be appointed are given as follows: L. Sicinius Velutus, son of Lucius, and L. Albinius Paterculus, son of Caius.

As for the rest of the passage here dealing with the reinstitution of the *tribuni* and the end of the rule of the *decemviri*, Cicero's own words are brief and clear: he merely fails to mention the name of the *decemvir* who granted ownership contrary to the claims of freedom, and of the father against whose daughter this decision was given. The *decemvir* of course was Appius Claudius, and the father of the girl L. Verginius. It now remains to explain the passage in which he speaks of the second withdrawal of the *plebs* and the restoration of harmony:

They then exchanged undertakings with three distinguished representatives and returned armed to Rome. They settled on the Aventine Hill, and then approached the Capitol, still armed; they appointed ten

Legati tres quorum nomina non ponit hi fuerunt: Sp.
Tarpeius, C. Iulius, P. Sulpicius, omnes consulares;
pontifex max. fuit M. Papirius.

*(78)   Etiam   haec   recentiora   praetereo: Porciam
principium   iustissimae   libertatis;   Cassiam   qua   lege
suffragiorum   ius   potestasque   convaluit;   alteram   Cassiam
quae populi iudicia firmavit.*
Quae sit illa lex Cassia qua suffragiorum potestas
convaluit manifestum est; nam ipse quoque paulo ante
dixit legem Cassium tulisse ut populus per tabellam
suffragium ferret.

Altera Cassia lex quae populi iudicia firmavit quae sit
potest quaeri. Est autem haec: L. Cassius L. f. Longinus
tribunus plebis C. Mario C. Flavio coss. plures leges ad
minuendam nobilitatis potentiam tulit, in quibus hanc etiam
ut quem populus damnasset cuive imperium abrogasset in
senatu ne esset. Tulerat autem eam maxime propter simultates cum Q. Servilio qui ante biennium consul fuerat et
cui populus, quia male adversus Cimbros rem gesserat,
imperium abrogavit.

Dicit de nobilibus:
*Qui   non   modo   cum   Sulla   verum   etiam   illo   mortuo
semper hoc per se summis opibus retinendum putaverunt,
inimicissimi C. Cottae fuerunt, quod is consul paulum
tribunis plebis non potestatis sed dignitatis addidit.*
Hic Cotta, ut puto vos reminisci, legem tulit ut
tribunis plebis liceret postea alios magistratus capere:
quod lege Sullae eis erat ademptum.

*Quam diu quidem hoc animo erga vos illa plebs erit
quo se ostendit esse, cum legem Aureliam, cum Rosciam
non modo accepit sed etiam efflagitavit.*
Aurelia lege communicata esse iudicia inter senatores
et equestrem ordinem et tribunos aerarios †quam L.
Roscius *(79)* Otho biennio ante confirmavit, in theatro ut

tribuni plebis *through the authority of the priest, there being no magistrate in office.*

The three unidentified representatives were named Sp. Tarpeius, C. Iulius, P. Sulpicius, all ex-consuls, and the priest M. Papirius.

(78) I will pass over more recent events also: the law of Porcius, fountainhead of freedom and justice; the law of Cassius, under which the principle and effect of the vote gained its standing; the second law of Cassius, which established the validity of decisions of the populus.

It is clear what this law of Cassius was (*137 B.C.*), under which the "effect of the vote gained its standing": Cicero has just remarked that Cassius passed a law enacting that the *populus* should cast their votes with tablets. The question is what this second law of Cassius was which "established the validity of decisions of the *populus*". Now L. Cassius Longinus, son of Lucius, as *tribunus plebis* (*104 B.C.*) carried a number of laws aimed at reducing the power of the *nobiles*, in particular that a man condemned by the *populus* or removed from office by them should not remain in the senate. This had come about because of his struggle with Q. Servilius, consul two years earlier, who had been removed from office by the *populus* owing to his poor performance against the Cimbri.

Concerning the *nobiles* Cicero says:

C. Cotta's greatest opponents were those who believed, not merely while Sulla was with them but after his death too, that they should retain control of this with all their strength; Cotta it was who restored to the tribuni plebis *some of their standing if not of their power.*

You no doubt remember that this Cotta carried a bill (*75 B.C.*) permitting *tribuni plebis* to proceed to further office, a course forbidden by the law of Sulla.

And the plebs *will continue to show the attitude to you, gentlemen, which it displayed in not merely accepting but demanding the laws of Aurelius and Roscius.*

The law of Aurelius (*70 B.C.*) shared the juries in court between senators, *equites*, and *tribuni aerarii*; *(79)* that of Roscius Otho, two years before this speech, gave

equitibus Romanis XIIII ordines spectandi gratia darentur.

Memoria teneo, cum primum senatores cum equitibus Romanis lege Plotia iudicarent, hominem dis ac nobilitati perinvisum Cn. Pompeium causam lege Varia de maiestate dixisse.

M. Plautius Silvanus tribunus plebis Cn. Pompeio Strabone L. Porcio Catone coss., secundo anno belli Italici cum equester ordo in iudiciis dominaretur, legem tulit adiuvantibus nobilibus; quae lex vim eam habuit quam Cicero significat: nam ex ea lege tribus singulae ex suo numero quinos denos suffragio creabant qui eo anno iudicarent. Ex eo factum est ut senatores quoque in eo numero esssent, et quidam etiam ex ipsa plebe.

PRO CORNELIO

Num in eo qui sint hi testes haesitatis? Ego vobis edam. Duo reliqui sunt de consularibus, inimici tribuniciae potestatis. Pauci praeterea adsentatores eorum atque adseculae subsequuntur.

M. Lucullum et M'. Lepidum significat. Quinque enim consulares, ut iam diximus, in Cornelium testimonium dixerunt: Q. Catulus, Q. Hortensius, Q. Metellus Pius pont. max., quos hac secunda oratione tractat, et duo qui nondum dixerant quos nunc significat Lucullus et Lepidus.

Quid? avunculus tuus clarissimus vir, clarissimo patre avo maioribus, credo, silentio, favente nobilitate, (80) nullo intercessore comparato populo Romano dedit et potentissimorum hominum conlegiis eripuit cooptandorum sacerdotum potestatem.

Hoc egere enarratione, quia hoc loco nomen non ponit quis fecerit, ei demum videri potest qui oblitus sit minus ante XX versus haec de eo ipso Ciceronem dixisse:

Sed si familiariter ex Q. Catulo sapientissimo viro atque humanissimo velim quaerere: utrius tandem tibi tribunatus minus probari potest, C. Corneli, an - non dicam P. Sulpici, non L. Saturnini, non Gai Gracchi, non Tiberi, neminem quem isti seditiosum existimant nominabo,

the *equites* the privilege in the theatre of occupying the
first fourteen rows of the audience.

I recall the occasion, as soon as equites *joined
senators on the juries under the law of Plotius, when Cn.
Pompeius, a man detested by both* nobiles *and gods,
pleaded on a charge of* maiestas *under the law of Varius.*

During the consulship of Cn. Pompeius Strabo and L.
Porcius Cato (*89 B.C.*), in the second year of the Italian
War, the *equites* were preponderant in the courts; then
the *tribunus plebis* M. Plautius Silvanus proposed a bill
with the support of the *nobiles:* the force of this bill is
as Cicero indicates. Each tribe was to elect fifteen men
from its members to serve as jurymen for that year. The
result was that this number included senators and some
persons also from the *plebs.*

ON BEHALF OF CORNELIUS[9]

*Do you feel any uncertainty about the identity of
these witnesses? Let me explain: there are two men from
the ranks of ex-consuls, being opponents of the power of
tribuni plebis. Besides them there are merely a few of
their attendants and sycophants.*

He means M. Lucullus and M'. Lepidus.[10] As I have
explained, five ex-consuls appeared for the prosecution in
the Cornelius case: Q. Catulus, Q. Hortensius, Q. Metellus
Pius the chief priest (Cicero deals with these men in this
second speech), and the two referred to here – Lucullus
and Lepidus – who had not yet made their statements.

*Now your uncle, an outstanding man with equally
outstanding father, grandfather, and forbears, removed
the power to appoint priests from the collegia of dominant
men and awarded it to the Roman populus, (80) without
any veto being attempted and presumably with the tacit
consent of the nobiles.*

Cicero does not say at this point who did this; but if
explanation is felt to be needed, it has no doubt been
forgotten that Cicero said the following about him twenty
lines previously:

*Supposing I were to ask the respected Q. Catulus in
a quite friendly manner the following question: whose*

sed avunculi tui, Q. Catule, clarissimi patriaeque amantissimi viri? quid mihi tandem responsurum putatis?

SEQVITVR

Quid? idem Domitius M. Silanum, consularem hominem, quem ad modum tr.pl. vexavit?

M. Silanus quinquennio ante consul fuerat quam Domitius tr.pl. esset, atque ipse quoque adversus Cimbros rem male gesserat: quam ob causam Domitius eum apud populum accusavit. Criminabatur rem cum Cimbris iniussu populi gessisse, idque principium fuisse calamitatum quas eo bello populus accepisset; ac de eo tabellam quoque edidit. Sed plenissime Silanus absolutus est; nam duae solae tribus eum, Sergia et Quirina, damnaverunt.

(81) Haec est controversia eius modi ut mihi probetur tr.pl. Cn. Domitius, Catulo M. Terpolius.

Contemptissimum nomen electum esse ex eis qui tr.pl. fuerant post infractam tribuniciam potestatem a Sulla, ante restitutam a Cn. Pompeio apparet. Fuit autem is tr.pl. ante XII annos D. Bruto et Mam. Lepido coss.; Cn. Domitius tribunus fuerat ante II de XL annos C. Mario II C. Fimbria coss.

Magno numero sententiarum Cornelius absolutus est.

tribunate is to be judged the less creditable - is it C. Cornelius' (and I will not include P. Sulpicius or L. Saturninus or Caius Gracchus or Tiberius Gracchus . . . none in fact that might be thought subversive) - or is it your uncle's, my dear Catulus, that outstanding and patriotic figure? Now what do you suppose he would say in reply?

And then:
Now consider the way in which this same Domitius harried the ex-consul M. Silanus.

M. Silanus had been consul (*109 B.C.*) five years before Domitius was *tribunus plebis*, and he too had performed poorly against the Cimbri; Domitius therefore prosecuted him before the *populus*. The allegation was that Silanus had conducted the campaign without the authority of the *populus*, and that this had been the origin of the disasters suffered by the *populus* in that war; a document too was produced by Domitius. However, Silanus was decisively acquitted, since no more than two tribes voted for conviction (Sergia and Quirina).

(81) The dispute between us is such that I approve of the tribunus plebis *Cn. Domitius, while Catulus' favourite is M. Terpolius.*

This last is the most worthless *tribunus plebis* elected between the humbling of tribunician power by Sulla and its restoration by Pompey: he was in office in the consulship of D. Brutus and Mam. Lepidus[11] twelve years previously *(77 B.C.)*: Cn. Domitius served 38 years earlier in the consulship of C. Marius (second time) and C. Fimbria (*104 B.C.*).

Cornelius secured acquittal by a decisive majority of the votes.

IN TOGA CANDIDA

[See R. Seager, "The first Catilinarian conspiracy",
Historia 1964, pp. 338ff., and "*Iusta Catilinae*", *Historia*
1973, pp. 240ff.]

The subject matter of this speech is thickly entangled
in controversy, largely as a result of the efforts of
Cicero himself and of Sallustius (see *Conspiracy of
Catiline*, tr. S. A. Handford); to make things still more
difficult to unravel, this speech of Cicero does not
survive independently, and only the fragments quoted
by Asconius are available to us.

The elections in 66 B.C. had undoubtedly been
controversial: after Catilina's unsuccessful attempt to
stand for the consulship (see A. p. 139), the two men
who were actually elected (P. Autronius and P. Sulla)
were charged with misconduct of their canvassing;
they were removed and replaced by L. Cotta and L.
Torquatus (see A. p. 137). These events are presumably one origin of the mysterious "First
Catilinarian Conspiracy" (A. pp. 131, 143), and there
is an echo in Asconius of Cicero's own allegation
(derived from the lost *Account of his Career*) that M.
Crassus was its chief instigator (A. p. 131; see also
Introduction to the *Pro Cornelio*, A. p. 87).

Now in 63 B.C., Cicero, the *novus homo*, was
enjoying his attainment of the office of consul at the
earliest possible age and in the face of powerful
opposition (see the *Exposition* below, p. 129). In
October/November he had succeeded in unearthing
damning circumstantial evidence that a subversive
conspiracy was indeed being actively promoted by
Catilina, whose third attempt at the consulship had
recently failed, and by an ally called C. Manlius, who
was busy exploiting grievances amongst the
population in Etruria. In his first speech *In Catilinam*
(see Cicero, *Selected Political Speeches*, tr. M. Grant),
Cicero allows himself some deliberately mysterious
references in front of the senate to Catilina having
planned to assassinate the consuls Cotta and Torquatus on their first day of office – 1 January 65.
These references are easily traceable to the more
ambitious hints about Catilina's guilt in the *In Toga*

Candida, and probably constitute the only remotely firm evidence for the "First Conspiracy". Sallustius' account duly introduces further participants in the affair. The question in fact whether the whole "First Conspiracy" was anything more than a scandalous rumour, unscrupulously put about by Cicero to obtain advantage in the consular election of 64 B.C., has been much discussed; see e.g. Scullard, *From the Gracchi to Nero*[5], pp. 105 ff.).

V. IN SENATV IN TOGA CANDIDA

CONTRA C. ANTONIVM ET
L. CATILINAM COMPETITORES

(82) Haec oratio dicta est L. Caesare C. Figulo coss. post annum quam pro Cornelio dixerat.

A R G V M E N T V M

Sex competitores in consulatus petitione Cicero habuit, duos patricios, P. Sulpicium Galbam, L. Sergium Catilinam; quattuor plebeios ex quibus duos nobiles, C. Antonium, M. Antoni oratoris filium, L. Cassium Longinum, duos qui tantum non primi ex familiis suis magistratum adepti erant, Q. Cornificium et C. Licinium Sacerdotem. Solus Cicero ex competitoribus equestri erat loco natus; atque in petitione patrem amisit.

Ceteri eius competitores modeste se gessere, visique sunt Q. Cornificius et Galba sobrii ac sancti viri, Sacerdos nulla improbitate notus; Cassius quamvis stolidus tum magis quam improbus videretur, post paucos menses in coniuratione Catilinae esse eum apparuit ac cruentissimarum sententiarum fuisse auctorem. Itaque hi quattuor prope iacebant.

Catilina autem et Antonius, *(83)* quamquam omnium maxime infamis eorum vita esset, tamen multum poterant. Coierant enim ambo ut Ciceronem consulatu deicerent, adiutoribus usi firmissimis M. Crasso et C. Caesare. Itaque haec oratio contra solos Catilinam et Antonium est. Causa orationis huius modi in senatu habendae Ciceroni fuit quod, cum in dies licentia ambitus augeretur propter praecipuam Catilinae et Antoni audaciam, censuerat senatus ut lex ambitus aucta etiam cum poena ferretur; eique rei Q. Mucius Orestinus tr.pl. intercesserat. Tum Cicero graviter senatu intercessionem ferente surrexit atque in coitionem Catilinae et Antoni invectus est ante dies comitiorum paucos.

V. *Speech delivered in the senate as candidate for the consulship, against his rivals C. Antonius and L. Catilina*

(82) This speech was delivered in the year of the consuls Lucius Caesar and Gaius Figulus *(64 B.C.)*, one year later than Cicero's speech on behalf of Cornelius.

EXPOSITION

Cicero had six rivals in his candidature for the consulship: two of these were *patricii* - P. Sulpicius Galba and L. Sergius Catilina - and four were *plebeii*. Of these, two belonged to *nobilis* families - C. Antonius,[1] son of the orator M. Antonius,[2] and L. Cassius Longinus - while two were almost the first of their respective *familiae* to reach public office, namely Q. Cornificius and C. Licinius Sacerdos. Cicero alone came from an equestrian family (incidentally he lost his father during the campaign). His rivals conducted their campaigns in a moderate manner: Cornificius and Galba presented themselves as respectable and sound men, and Sacerdos had no known villainy to his credit. Cassius seemed to be more a half-wit than a villain, though some months later he turned up in Catilina's conspiracy voicing the most bloodthirsty proposals. These four men were in fact a hopeless electoral prospect.

As for Catilina and Antonius, *(83)* their lives had been spectacularly disreputable, but they had a good deal of influence. They had made a pact to frustrate Cicero's candidature, with the energetic support of M. Crassus and C. Caesar; hence this present speech attacks only Catilina and Antonius. The occasion of the speech was as follows: Catilina's and Antonius' reckless behaviour had brought about an increase in flagrant bribery, and the senate had considered a proposal that a law on corruption should be passed, with enhanced penalties. Q. Mucius Orestinus, *tribunus plebis*, had vetoed the proposal, and then, as the senate clearly resented this use of the veto, Cicero rose to his feet and, shortly before the elections were due, attacked the pact between Catilina and Antonius.

ENARRATIO

Dico, P.C., superiore nocte cuiusdam hominis nobilis et valde in hoc largitionis quaestu noti et cogniti domum Catilinam et Antonium cum sequestribus suis convenisse.

Aut C. Caesaris aut M. Crassi domum significat. Ei enim acerrimi ac potentissimi fuerunt Ciceronis refragatores cum petiit consulatum, quod eius in dies civilem crescere dignitatem animadvertebant: et hoc ipse Cicero in expositione consiliorum suorum significat; eius quoque coniurationis quae Cotta et Torquato coss. ante annum quam haec dicerentur facta est a Catilina et Pisone arguit M. Crassum auctorem fuisse.

Quem enim aut amicum habere potest is qui tot (84) civis trucidavit, aut clientem qui in sua civitate cum peregrino negavit se iudicio aequo certare posse?

Dicitur Catilina, cum in Sullanis partibus fuisset, crudeliter fecisse. Nominatim etiam postea Cicero dicit quos occiderit, Q. Caecilium, M. Volumnium, L. Tanusium. M. etiam Mari Gratidiani summe popularis hominis, qui ob id bis praetor fuit, caput abscisum per urbem sua manu Catilina tulerat: quod crimen saepius ei tota oratione obicit. Fuerat vero hic Gratidianus arta necessitudine Ciceroni coniunctus.

Clientem autem negavit habere posse C. Antonium: nam is multos in Achaia spoliaverat nactus de exercitu Sullano equitum turmas. Deinde Graeci qui spoliati erant eduxerunt Antonium in ius ad M. Lucullum praetorem qui ius inter peregrinos dicebat. Egit pro Graecis C. Caesar etiam tum adulescentulus, de quo paulo ante mentionem fecimus; et cum Lucullus id quod Graeci postulabant decrevisset, appellavit tribunos Antonius iuravitque se ideo eiurare quod aequo iure uti non posset. Hunc Antonium Gellius et Lentulus censores sexennio quo haec dicerentur senatu moverunt titulosque subscripserunt, quod socios diripuerit, quod iudicium recusarit, quod propter aeris alieni magnitudinem praedia manciparit bonaque sua in potestate non habeat.

C O M M E N T A R Y

I assert, gentlemen, that last night Catilina and Antonius, with their attendants, met at the house of a certain nobilis *individual well known to investigations of extravagance.*

He means the house of either Caesar or Crassus, since during Cicero's candidature these two were his fiercest and most forceful assailants, and they were aware that his public reputation was growing steadily. Indeed Cicero makes this clear in his own account of his career. Furthermore, he asserts that M. Crassus instigated the conspiracy which was formed by Catilina and Piso in the year before this speech was delivered.[3]

Can anyone be a friend of a man who has murdered so many citizens, (84) can anyone be a client of a man who has said he could not, in his own country, meet a foreigner in court and fight the case with him on equal terms?

When Catilina was one of Sulla's group of supporters, he acted – we are told – very cruelly. Cicero actually goes on to list his victims – Q. Caecilius, M. Volumnius, L. Tanusius. And M. Marius Gratidianus, who was twice elected praetor because of his appeal to the voters, had his head lopped off by Catilina and carried round the city by his assassin. This allegation is made against him many times during the present speech; and this Gratidianus was by the way a close relative of Cicero.

Cicero remarks that no-one could be a client of Antonius: the latter had in fact acquired a troop of horse from Sulla's army and used it to rob a large number of persons in Greece. These Greek victims then brought Antonius to court in front of L. Lucullus, the praetor responsible for cases involving aliens. Counsel for the Greeks was the young C. Caesar mentioned earlier. When Lucullus gave judgment for the Greeks, Antonius summoned the help of *tribuni plebis* and announced he was withdrawing because he could not expect justice. Now six years before the present speech was delivered, this Antonius had been removed from the senate by the *censores* Gellius and Lentulus, with the explanation that he had robbed provincial citizens, shown contempt of court, mortgaged his estates on account of debt, and was not in full ownership of his property.

(85) Nec senatum respexit cum gravissimis vestris decretis absens notatus est.

Catilina ex praetura Africam provinciam obtinuit: quam cum graviter vexasset, legati Afri in senatu iam tum absente illo questi sunt, multaeque graves sententiae in senatu de eo dictae sunt.

In iudiciis quanta vis esset didicit cum est absolutus: si aut illud iudicium aut illa absolutio nominanda est.

Ante annum quam haec dicerentur Catilina, cum redisset ex Africa Torquato et Cotta coss., accusatus est repetundarum a P. Clodio adulescente, qui postea inimicus Ciceronis fuit.

Defensus est Catilina, ut Fenestella tradit, a M. Cicerone. Quod ego ut addubitem haec ipsa Ciceronis oratio facit, maxime quod is nullam mentionem rei habet, cum potuerit invidiam facere competitori tam turpiter adversus se coeunti: praesertim cum alterum competitorem suum Antonium in eadem hac oratione sua admoneat suo beneficio eum ex ultimo loco praeturae candidatum ad tertium pervenisse.

Nescis me praetorem primum esse factum, te concessione competitorum et collatione centuriarum et meo maxime beneficio ex postremo in tertium locum esse subiectum?

Qui igitur Antonio suffragationem suam imputandam putat, is si defendisset Catilinam, caput eius protectum a se nonne imputaret? Quod ita esse manifestum est ex eo quod statim dicit. Q. enim Mucius tr.pl. intercedebat *(86)* ne lex ambitus ferretur; quod facere pro Catilina videbatur.

Hunc Mucium in hac oratione Cicero appellans sic ait:

Te tamen, Q. Muci, tam male de populo Romano existimare moleste fero qui hesterno die me esse dignum consulatu negabas. Quid? p.R. minus diligenter sibi constitueret defensorem quam tu tibi? Cum tecum furti L. Calenus ageret, me potissimum fortunarum tuarum patronum esse voluisti. Cuius tute consilium in tua turpissima causa delegisti, hunc honestissimarum rerum defensorem p.R. auctore te repudiare potest? Nisi forte

(85) . . . and he has taken no notice of the reprimand given in his absence by you, gentlemen, in the strongest terms.

After his term as praetor Catilina was granted the province of Africa. He proved most repressive there, and while he was still away from Rome a deputation complained about him in the senate, whereupon a number of senators spoke about him unfavourably.

His acquittal demonstrated to him the power of the courts – if, that is, one can use the words "court" or "acquittal" in this context.

The year before this speech was delivered, Catilina on his return from Africa in the consulship of Torquatus and Cotta *(65 B.C.)* was prosecuted for *repetundae* by P. Clodius, the young man who was later Cicero's enemy. Fenestella tells us that Cicero spoke for the defence, but I hesitate to believe that, especially because Cicero does not mention such a thing, when by so doing he could have damaged the repute of a rival candidate who had now entered into a contemptible pact against him. Indeed in this present speech he points out that Antonius, his other rival, owed his rise from bottom to third place in the praetorian elections to Cicero himself:

Are you unaware that I came first in the elections for praetor, while you just managed to come third owing to your rivals' indulgence, the connivance of the voters, and most of all my generous assistance?

A man who took the credit for getting Antonius elected would surely take the credit for saving Catilina, if he had spoken in his defence. This is clear from what he goes on to say. It was Q. Mucius the *tribunus plebis (86)* who vetoed the proposal to legislate against bribery – a step taken for the benefit of Catilina. Now Cicero in the present speech addresses Mucius like this:

I resent, Mucius, your showing a low opinion of the Roman populus in saying yesterday that I did not deserve the consulship. I ask you, would the populus be less careful in choosing its defender than you would be in choosing your own? When Calenus charged you with theft, you particularly asked that I should speak on your behalf: is it now possible for the Roman populus to repudiate at your suggestion the defender of their

hoc dicturus es, quo tempore cum L. Caleno furti
depectus sis, eo tempore in me tibi parum esse auxili
vidisse.

Vere cum egerit Muci causam Cicero sicut Catilinae
egisse eum videri vult Fenestella, cur iam quamvis male
existimet de causa Muci, tamen ei exprobret patrocinium
suum, non idem in Catilina faciat, si modo pro eo dixit? et
cur ipsum illud iudicium saepius in infamiam vocat? quod
parcius videtur fuisse facturus, si in eo iudicio fuisset
patronus.

Atque ut alia omittam, hoc certe vix videtur dicturus
fuisse, si illo patrono Catilina repetundarum absolutus
esset:
Stupris se omnibus ac flagitiis contaminavit; caede
nefaria cruentavit; diripuit socios; leges quaestiones
iudicia violavit - et postea:

Quid ego ut violaveris provinciam praedicem? Nam ut
te illic gesseris non audeo dicere, quoniam **(87)** *absolutus*
es. Mentitos esse equites Romanos, falsas fuisse tabellas
honestissimae civitatis existimo, mentitum Q. Metellum Pium,
mentitam Africam: vidisse puto nescio quid illos iudices
qui te innocentem iudicarunt. O miser qui non sentias illo
iudicio te non absolutum verum ad aliquod severius iudi-
cium ac maius supplicium reservatum!
Verine ergo simile est haec eum Catilinae obicere, si
illo defendente absolutus esset? Praeterea movet me quod,
cum sint commentarii Ciceronis causarum, eius tamen
defensionis nullum est commentarium aut principium.

Ita quidem iudicio absolutus est Catilina ut Clodius
infamis fuerit praevaricatus esse: nam et reiectio iudicum
ad arbitrium rei videbatur esse facta.

Populum vero cum inspectante populo collum secuit
hominis maxime popularis quanti faceret ostendit.
Diximus et paulo ante Mari caput Catilinam per urbem
tulisse.

Me qua amentia inductus sit ut contemneret con-
stituere non possum. Vtrum aequo animo laturum putavit?
At in suo familiarissimo viderat me ne aliorum quidem

honour, whose advice you sought at your disreputable trial? . . . unless that is you propose to argue that when you entered into collusion with Calenus, you found in me little assistance for your cause.

Cicero did indeed speak on Mucius' behalf, and Fenestella would have us believe that he did for Catilina too. Now although Cicero feels contempt for Mucius' case, he nevertheless draws attention to the patronage he offered; why then does he not do the same in the case of Catilina, if he did indeed speak for him? Why further does he frequently pour contempt on the verdict? He would hardly be likely to do that if he had been a sponsor on that occasion. In short, he would not be likely to assert the following if Catilina had been acquitted of *repetundae* through his sponsorship:

He has befouled himself with all manner of immorality and villainy, he has stained himself with the most wicked bloodshed, he has robbed the provincials, he has done violence to laws, judicial processes, courts. . .

What am I to say about the violence you did to your province? I dare not talk of your conduct there, (87) since you were acquitted. In my view the jurors, the voting tablets, Q. Metellus Pius, Africa itself, were all liars. But I do believe the jurors who acquitted you were aware of something. Poor fellow, you who fail to realize you were not acquitted by that verdict, but saved up for some more savage verdict, for a worse fate.

Is it likely that he would have hurled this abuse at Catilina if he had defended him on the occasion of his acquittal? Another powerful consideration is that while notes of Cicero's cases are extant, there is no note or even preliminary work on this defence. The acquittal of Catilina incidentally aroused the rumour that Clodius had colluded, since the business of rejecting potential jurors appeared to be conducted according to the defendant's wishes.

He displayed his opinion of the populus *when he severed the neck of a most* popularis *man before an audience of the* populus.

As I said earlier, Catilina carried round the city the head of Marius Gratidianus.

I cannot conceive what insanity led him to disregard my claims. Did he imagine I would not mind? . . . when he

iniurias mediocriter posse ferre.
Manifestum est C. Verrem significari.

Alter pecore omni vendito et saltibus prope addictis pastores retinet, ex quibus ait se cum velit subito fugitivorum bellum excitaturum.
C. Antonium significat.

(88) Alter induxit eum quem potuit ut repente gladiatores populo non debitos pollicerentur; eos ipse consularis candidatus perspexit et legit et emit; id praesente populo Romano factum est.
Q. Gallium, quem postea reum ambitus defendit, significare videtur. Hic enim cum esset praeturae candidatus, quod in aedilitate quam ante annum gesserat bestias non habuerat, dedit gladiatorium munus sub titulo patri se id dare.

Quam ob rem augete etiam mercedem, si voltis, Q. Muci ut perseveret legem impedire, ut coepit senatus consultum; sed ego ea lege contentus sum qua duos consules designatos uno tempore damnari vidimus.
Legem Calpurniam significat quam C. Calpurnius Piso ante triennium de ambitu tulerat. Quod dicit autem damnatos esse designatos consules, P. Sullam et P. Autronium, de quibus iam diximus, vult intellegi.

Cognomen autem Q. Mucio tribuno quem nominat fuit Orestinus.

Atque ut istum omittam in exercitu Sullano praedonem, in introitu gladiatorem, in victoria quadrigarium.
De Antonio dici manifestum est. Dicit eum *in exercitu Sullae praedonem* propter equitum turmas quibus Achaiam ab eo vexatam esse significavimus; *in introitu gladiatorem* pertinet ad invidiam proscriptionis quae tum facta est; *in victoria quadrigarium,* quod cum Sulla post victoriam circenses faceret ita ut honesti homines quadrigas agitarent, fuit inter eos C. Antonius.

*had already seen that I could not tolerate the injustice
done even to outsiders in the case of that great friend of
his.*

Clearly he means C. Verres.

*One of these two has sold off all his herds and
assigned his estates, but is keeping his farm labourers,
saying that from them he will deploy an army of deser-
ters at once when he chooses.*

Antonius is referred to.

(88) *The other persuaded a man who was open to this
persuasion to promise a show of gladiators to the populus
when this was not required. He, the consular candidate,
personally inspected, chose, and purchased these gladiators, in front of the Roman populus.*

The person referred to is Q. Gallius, whom he
afterwards defended on a charge of bribery. While he was
aedilis a year earlier, this Gallius had presented no
beast-fight; so when his candidature for the praetorship
arrived he did present a gladiatorial show, with the
advertisement stating that it was a present for his father.

*Therefore if you wish increase Mucius' reward for
maintaining his opposition to the bill as he has to the
senate's resolution. Personally I am satisfied with the law
under which we have seen two consuls-elect convicted
together.*

He is referring to the law on bribery promoted by C.
Calpurnius Piso three years earlier: the reference to the
conviction of consuls-elect is to P. Sulla and P. Autronius,
who were mentioned earlier. Q. Mucius, the *tribunus
plebis* alluded to, had as his third name Orestinus.

*I forbear to mention then this ruffian in Sulla's army,
this cut-throat at the entry into Rome, this charioteer at
the victory parade.*

Clearly a reference to Antonius. He says "a ruffian in
Sulla's army" on account of the troop of horse with
which, as I have explained, he terrorized Greece. "This
cut-throat at the entry into Rome" is an allusion to the
outrage caused by the proscriptions then taking place.
"Charioteer at the victory parade" reminds us that Sulla
held races after his victory, with distinguished men
taking part as riders, including Antonius.

(89) Te vero, Catilina, consulatum sperare aut cogitare non prodigium atque portentum est? A quibus enim petis? A principibus civitatis? qui tibi, cum L. Volcacio cos. in consilio fuissent, ne petendi quidem potestatem esse voluerunt.

Paulo ante diximus Catilinam, cum de provincia Africa decederet petiturus consulatum et legati Afri questi de eo in senatu graviter essent, supervenisse. Professus deinde est Catilina petere se consulatum. L. Volcacius Tullus consul consilium publicum habuit an rationem Catilinae habere deberet, si peteret consulatum: nam quaerebatur repetundarum. Catilina ob eam causam destitit a petitione.

A senatoribus? qui te auctoritate sua spoliatum ornamentis omnibus vinctum paene Africanis oratoribus tradiderunt?

Diximus modo de hoc. Nam iudicium quoque secutum est repetundarum, quo ipse per infamiam liberatus est Catilina, sed ita ut senatorum urna damnaret, equitum et tribunorum absolveret.

Ab equestri ordine? quem trucidasti?

Equester ordo pro Cinnanis partibus contra Sullam steterat, multique pecunias abstulerant: ex quo saccularii erant appellati, atque ob eius rei invidiam post Sullanam victoriam erant interfecti.

A plebe? cui spectaculum eius modi tua crudelitas praebuit, ut te nemo sine gemitu ac recordatione luctus aspicere possit?

(90) Eiusdem illius Mari Gratidiani quod caput gestarit obicit.

Quo loco dicit Catilinam caput M. Mari gestasse:

Quod caput etiam tum plenum animae et spiritus ad Sullam usque ab Ianiculo ad aedem Apollinis manibus ipse suis detulit.

Omnia sunt manifesta. Ne tamen erretis, quod his temporibus aedes Apollinis in Palatio fuit nobilissima, admonendi estis non hanc a Cicerone significari, utpote quam post mortem etiam Ciceronis multis annis Imp. Caesar, quem nunc Divum Augustum dicimus, post Actiacam victoriam fecerit: sed illam demonstrari quae est extra portam Carmentalem inter forum holitorium et circum Flaminium. Ea enim sola tum quidem Romae Apollinis aedes.

(89) Truly it is a monstrous phenomenon that you, Catilina, should expect or indeed consider the consulship. Who will grant it to you? Our leading men of the state? When they acted as advisers to L. Volcacius the consul, they refused you permission even to stand for election.

As I said earlier, Catilina returned from his province of Africa to stand for the consulship, and arrived home after a deputation from Africa had laid serious complaints about him in the senate. Catilina then declared his wish to stand. L. Volcacius Tullus the consul held an open discussion as to whether Catilina's application should be granted, since he was under investigation for *repetundae*. As a result Catilina abandoned his attempt.[4]

Will the senate? They stripped you by their authority of all your insignia and passed you all but handcuffed to the representatives from Africa.

I have explained this already. The trial for *repetundae* followed, and Catilina was scandalously acquitted, but only on the votes of *equites* and *tribuni aerarii*, since the senators' votes were for conviction.

Will the equites, who were your victims?

The *equites* had supported Cinna's group against Sulla, and many of them had taken away their money with them; hence they were called "handbags". Because of the feelings this aroused, they were put to death after Sulla's victory.

Will the plebs? They were offered through your viciousness a show which prevents anyone from looking upon you without a cry of grief remembered.

(90) He is speaking once more of the occasion when Catilina brandished the head of Marius Gratidianus. In the following excerpt he describes how Catilina did so:

This head still alive and breathing he carried to Sulla in his own hands all the way from the Ianiculan hill to the temple of Apollo.

This is quite clear. To avoid misunderstanding I must point out that the splendid temple of Apollo nowadays sited on the Palatine is not the one referred to by Cicero. That temple was built many years after Cicero's death by Caesar, now called Augustus the God, following the victory at Actium. The one referred to here is outside the Carmentalis gate between the Forum Holitorium and the

Loquitur cum Catilina:

Quid tu potes in defensione tua dicere quod illi non dixerint? at illi multa dixerunt quae tibi dicere non licebit –

et paulo post:

Denique illi negare potuerunt et negaverunt: tu tibi ne infitiandi quidem impudentiae locum reliquisti. Qua re praeclara dicentur iudicia tulisse si, qui infitiantem Luscium condemnarunt, Catilinam absolverint confitentem.

Hic quem nominat L. Luscius, notus centurio Sullanus divesque e victoria factus – nam amplius centies possederat – damnatus erat non multo ante quam Cicero dixit. Obiectae *(91)* sunt ei tres caedes proscriptorum.

Circa eosdem dies L. quoque Bellienus damnatus est quem Cicero ait avunculum esse Catilinae. Hic autem Lucretium Ofellam consulatum contra voluntatem Sullae ad turbandum statum civitatis petentem occiderat iussu Sullae tunc dictatoris. His ergo negat ignotum esse, cum et imperitos se homines esse et, si quem etiam interfecissent, imperatori ac dictatori paruisse dicerent, ac negare quoque possent: Catilinam vero infitiari non posse. Huius autem criminis periculum quod obicit Cicero paucos post menses Catilina subiit. Post effecta enim comitia consularia et Catilinae repulsam fecit eum reum inter sicarios L. Lucceius paratus eruditusque, qui postea consulatum quoque petiit.

Hanc tu habes dignitatem qua fretus me contemnis et despicis, an eam quam reliqua in vita es consecutus? cum ita vixisti ut non esset locus tam sanctus quo non adventus tuus, etiam cum culpa nulla subesset, crimen afferret.

Fabia virgo Vestalis causam incesti dixerat, cum ei Catilina obiceretur, eratque absoluta. Haec Fabia quia soror erat Terentiae Ciceronis, ideo sic dixit:

etiam si culpa nulla subesset.

Ita et suis pepercit et nihilo levius inimico summi opprobrii turpitudinem obiecit.

Circus Flaminius. At the time this was the only temple of Apollo at Rome. Now he addresses Catilina:

What can you say in your own defence that they have not said? In fact they have said much that you may not say.

And then:

They were in a position to say no, and they did. But you have left yourself no chance even to deny your appalling guilt. It will be a truly admirable verdict if those who convicted Luscius in the face of his denial acquit Catilina in the face of his admission.

This man L. Luscius was a well-known centurion in Sulla's army who prospered through the victory with a fortune of more than ten million *sestertii*, and had been convicted, shortly before Cicero delivered this speech, *(91)* for the murder of three proscribed men. At about that time L. Bellienus, said by Cicero to be Catilina's uncle, was also convicted. He had murdered Lucretius Ofella, who was standing for the consulship against Sulla's wishes with intent to foment unrest; this murder was done on the instructions of Sulla who was then *dictator*. Cicero is saying that they did not escape proceedings; they said they were purely amateurs, and any deaths they might have caused were carried out in obedience to a man who was commander and *dictator*; they were equally in a position to deny their crimes. But Catilina could not make a denial. Moreover, he did stand trial a few months later for the offence which Cicero alleges; for after the consular elections were over and Catilina failed to gain election he was prosecuted for murder by L. Lucceius, a learned and well-equipped politician who later on stood for the consulship himself.

Is your reputation such as to entitle you to disregard and ignore me, or is it such as you have acquired by your conduct hitherto? Certainly your way of life has ensured that nowhere is safe from the accusation, if not guilt, which your arrival brings with it.

The Vestal Virgin Fabia had defended a charge of incest, involving Catilina, and had been acquitted. Cicero remarks "if not guilt" because Fabia was the sister of his own wife Terentia, thus sparing his own family unpleasantness and at the same time ensuring that his opponent feels the full weight of the charge of immorality.

Cum deprehendebare in adulteriis, cum deprehendebas adulteros ipse, cum ex eodem stupro tibi et uxorem et filiam invenisti.

Dicitur Catilina adulterium commisisse cum ea quae ei postea socrus fuit, et ex eo natam stupro duxisse uxorem, *(92)* cum filia eius esset. Hoc Lucceius quoque Catilinae obicit in orationibus quas in eum scripsit. Nomina harum mulierum nondum inveni.

Quid ego ut violaveris provinciam praedicem, cuncto populo Romano clamante ac resistente? nam ut te illic gesseris non audeo dicere, quoniam absolutus es.

Dictum est iam saepius Catilinam ex praetura Africam obtinuisse et accusante eum repetundarum P. Clodio absolutum esse.

Praetereo nefarium illum conatum tuum et paene acerbum et luctuosum rei publicae diem, cum Cn. Pisone socio, ne quem alium nominem, caedem optimatum facere voluisti.

Quos non nominet intellegitis. Fuit enim opinio Catilinam et Cn. Pisonem, adulescentem perditum, coniurasse ad caedem senatus faciendam ante annum quam haec dicta sunt, Cotta et Torquato coss., eamque caedem ideo non esse factam quod prius quam parati essent coniuratis signum dedisset Catilina.

Piso autem, cum haec dicerentur, perierat, in Hispaniam missus a senatu per honorem legationis ut †auus suus ablegaretur. Ibi quidem dum iniurias provincialibus facit, occisus erat, ut quidam credebant, a Cn. Pompeii clientibus Pompeio non invito.

An oblitus es te ex me, cum praeturam peteremus, petisse ut tibi primum locum concederem? Quod cum saepius ageres et impudentius a me (93) contenderes, meministi me tibi respondere impudenter te facere qui id a me peteres quod a te Boculus numquam impetrasset?

Diximus iam supra Sullae ludis quos hic propter victoriam fecerit quadrigas C. Antonium et alios quosdam nobiles homines agitasse. Praeterea Antonius redemptas habebat ab aerario vectigales quadrigas, quam redemptionem senatori habere licet per legem. Fuit autem notissimus in circo quadrigarum agitator Boculus.

When you were discovered in adultery, when you personally uncovered adultery, when you made one woman both wife and daughter by a single sinful act.

It is said that Catilina committed adultery with the woman who was later on his mother-in-law, and that he married the woman born of this relationship, *(92)* who was consequently his daughter. Lucceius too makes this allegation against Catilina in the invectives he wrote about him. I have not yet discovered the names of these two women.

What am I to say about the violence you did to your province, against the opposition of the entire Roman populus? I dare not talk about your conduct there, since you were acquitted.

To repeat: Catilina governed Africa as his province after the praetorship, was prosecuted by P. Clodius for *repetundae*, and acquitted.

I will omit to mention that criminal enterprise of yours, which very nearly brought about agony and suffering to our country – that occasion when you planned the massacre of optimates *in company with Cn. Piso, to name but one.*

You no doubt realize who are the unnamed individuals.[5] It was supposed that Catilina and Piso, a depraved young man, plotted to massacre the senate a year previously, and that this massacre failed to take place because Catilina gave his associates the signal before they were ready.[6] When the present speech was delivered, Piso had been sent to Spain by the senate on an official mission . . . (?) and had died there. He met his death while harassing the local inhabitants, allegedly at the hands of Pompey's agents with Pompey's acquiescence.

Have you forgotten that when we stood for the praetorship you asked me to surrender first place to you? You persisted in this shameless request, (93) and I remarked on your impudence in requesting me to grant what Boculus never secured from you.

I have said above that at Sulla's victory celebrations C. Antonius and other *nobiles* drove in chariot races. Furthermore, Antonius had bought from the treasury some rented chariots (the senate being legally entitled to negotiate such a deal). Boculus was a famous charioteer in

Dicit de malis civibus:

Qui postea quam illo quo conati erant Hispaniensi pugiunculo nervos incidere civium Romanorum non potue- runt, duas uno tempore conantur in rem publicam sicas destringere.

Hispaniensem pugiunculum Cn. Pisonem appellat, quem in Hispania occisum esse dixi. Duas sicas Catilinam et Antonium appellari manifestum est.

Hunc vos scitote Licinium gladiatorem iam immisisse capillum Catilinae †iudic. quā Q. ue Curium hominem quaestorium.

Curius hic notissimus fuit aleator, damnatusque postea est. In hunc est hendecasyllabus Calvi elegans:

Et talos Curius pereruditus.

Huic orationi Ciceronis et Catilina et Antonius contumeliose responderunt, quod solum poterant, invecti in *(94)* novitatem eius. Feruntur quoque orationes nomine illorum editae, non ab ipsis scriptae sed ab Ciceronis obtrectatoribus: quas nescio an satius sit ignorare. Ceterum Cicero consul omnium consensu factus est: Antonius pauculis centuriis Catilinam superavit, cum ei propter patris nomen paulo speciosior manus suffragata esset quam Catilinae.

the circus.

He now remarks of certain vicious citizens:

They attempted to sever the sinews of Roman citizens with their Spanish dagger and failed; now they are trying to plunge two knives simultaneously into our country.

"Spanish dagger" refers to Piso, killed in Spain. Clearly the "two knives" are Catilina and Antonius.

You must realize that Licinius, that gladiator, has grown Catilina's hair (?) † . . . † *the ex-quaestor Curius.*

Curius was a notorious gambler, afterwards convicted. Here is a neat hendecasyllabic line alluding to him, written by Calvus:

And there's Curius, every inch a scholar.

Catilina and Antonius made an offensive reply to this speech of Cicero's, and chose the only course they could: *(94)* to attack his lack of distinguished background. Certain other speeches were put out under their names, written not by them but by Cicero's enemies: better perhaps to leave them aside. At all events Cicero gained the consulship by a clear majority: Antonius led Catilina by the votes of a few centuries, since his father's reputation gave him the advantage of a more distinguished body of supporters than Catilina's.

IN PISONEM: NOTES

¹ There is a gap in the MSS. here. It has been suggested that the missing authority is Fenestella, but the name of Cicero's secretary and former slave, Tiro (proposed by Kiessling-Schöll), has the advantage of fitting the space of four or five characters: and as well as editing Cicero's speeches, he wrote a biography of him (see *pro Milone*, A. p. 75).

² By the law of the *tribunus plebis* P. Vatinius, 59 B.C., C. Iulius Caesar was granted Cisalpine Gaul as his province for a term of five years. Caesar's political opponents had made strenuous (though in the end unsuccessful) efforts to ensure that he would not be allocated any promising province, even to the extent of reserving what Scullard calls a "forestry commission" for the successful candidates for the consulship of 59 B.C..

³ See Appendix, A. p. 152, for a note on this mistaken statement.

⁴ On the foundation of Placentia (modern *Piacenza*) see Polybius 3.40 and Livius *epitome* 20. Asconius may be raising a non-existent problem here, since colonies which enjoyed "Latin" rights were granted the status of *municipium* after the "Social War" in 90 or 89 B.C.. For further information, see Appendix, A. p. 152, and *OCD²* s.v. *municipium*.

⁵ Born P. Cornelius Dolabella, but adopted by a P. Cornelius Lentulus into his *plebeius* family so that he was eligible for the office of *tribunus plebis*, which he held in 47 B.C. In the Index below he is listed under his full name – P. Cornelius Lentulus Dolabella. In fact Asconius has omitted mention of Furius Crassipes, whom Cicero's daughter married after the death of C. Piso in 57 (she was certainly engaged to Crassipes in 56 (Cicero, *Letters to his brother Quintus* 2.4.2), and married Dolabella probably in 51, when Cicero was abroad as governor of Cilicia).

⁶ See Cicero, *In Catilinam* I.2.4.

⁷ I have translated here the wording of the so-called *senatus consultum ultimum*, a measure first passed in 121 B.C. at the request of the consul Opimius in order to deal with the challenge of C. Gracchus, the *tribunus plebis*. It was used several times after this date, notably in 100 B.C. by the consul C. Marius against the *tribunus plebis*

Saturninus; the death of Saturninus remained highly controversial. In 63 B.C. the whole issue was revived when charges were brought against C. Rabirius, now an old man, who had allegedly been involved in the action of 100 B.C. Cicero, in his defence of Rabirius, upheld the *SCU* (see Glossary, s.v. *perduellio*), and himself exploited the measure later in 63 B.C. during his efforts to frustrate the insurrection of Catilina. It is unlikely that it actually granted the consuls or anyone else any extraordinary powers (and did not therefore resemble exactly a declaration of martial law); rather it perhaps embodied a less specific assertion of moral support of the consuls by their colleagues in the senate during a time of serious stress.

⁸ I have adopted Shackleton Bailey's proposal and printed *Cloelius* for the MS. *Clodius* throughout: see Preface above p. v.

⁹ There are two likely possibilities who were *tribuni plebis* in 60 B.C.: L. Flavius and C. Herennius. Flavius was the author of a proposal to make land available for the veterans of Pompey's army after its return from the war against Mithridates in Asia Minor, while Herennius was engaged in promoting the transfer of the *patricius* P. Clodius to the *plebs.* Both of them seem to have come into conflict with Metellus Celer in the process.

¹⁰ The reference here is to legislation (probably two separate laws, of Aelius and Fufius) passed in about 150 B.C. The law of Aelius seems to have upheld the right of a holder of a magistracy to prevent legislative assemblies being convened: he did this by announcing in advance that he would be observing the heavens for omens. It was this very device that had been used in 59 B.C. by Iulius Caesar's colleague M. Calpurnius Bibulus to try to obstruct legislation by Caesar.

¹¹ Presumably a reference, in spite of the "already", to the Commentary below on *In toga candida*, A. pp. 133f.

¹² See Cicero, *De lege agraria* 2.34.94 (63 B.C.).

¹³ In 109 B.C. a special *quaestio* was established by the *tribunus plebis* C. Mamilius Limetanus; its task was to investigate alleged acts of treason by certain *nobiles* during the war against Iugurtha (for details see Sallustius, *Iugurtha* 40.1-2). The jury was to consist wholly of *equites*, who had gained participation in the jury-courts by legislation of C. Gracchus in 123/2 B.C. Opimius himself had led a commission to attempt a resolution of

problems in Numidia: this enterprise later collapsed, and Opimius was alleged to have taken bribes from Iugurtha.

PRO SCAVRO: NOTES

[1] Normally the consular elections would have taken place within the next week or two, but this time they were repeatedly postponed, and were held finally as late as July 53. Things were no better the following year: see *pro Milone*, A. p. 51.

[2] A man who had been designated as consul at the elections (normally in July) would be immune from prosecution (like those actually in office) until the end of his term; the sole exception to this rule seems to be a prosecution for irregular conduct of an electoral campaign (e.g. the case of the men originally elected consuls in 66 B.C., see *In toga candida*, A. p. 137).

[3] The legislator could be Iulius Caesar (who certainly promoted legislation on the composition of juries in 46 B.C.) or the emperor Augustus in 17 B.C. (so A. H. M. Jones, *Criminal Courts of the Roman Republic and Principate*, 1972, p. 64).

[4] Clark, following Madvig, brackets this whole comment as spurious. Certainly it is unique in Asconius' surviving text in being a purely grammatical discussion; nevertheless, since Asconius was writing for his sons (A. p. 69), he may have thought it would do them good.

[5] i.e. C. Iulius Caesar, the future *dictator.*

PRO MILONE: NOTES

[1] See Asconius' comment on an extract (A. pp. 81f.) from this speech, which seems to be the source of his remark here.

[2] This extraordinary woman deserves a special mention for her resourcefulness, her power of survival, and the identity of her three husbands, who were (in chronological order) P. Clodius Pulcher, C. Scribonius Curio the younger, and M. Antonius (Mark Antony). See the appreciative description of this "Amazon" in J. P. V. D. Balsdon, *Roman Women*, 1962, pp. 49f. She is not the same person as the Fulvia who was implicated in Catilina's conspiracy in 63 B.C.

[3] Before the Roman calendar was reformed during Iulius Caesar's dictatorship (46 B.C. - the beginning of the so-called "Julian Calendar"), the Roman year consisted of 354 days (12 lunar cycles); it was adjusted to the solar year by periodically inserting an extra month, the decision to intercalate being taken by the priests. (The matter was frequently handled unsystematically, and by 46 B.C. a discrepancy of some 90 days had built up between the calendar and solar year.) The intercalary month probably began on the day after 23 February, and individual days were identified in the usual way by counting back from the next named day - in this case the Kalends (first day) of March. The wording of Asconius here also suggests incidentally that the intercalary "absorbed" the remaining days of February in its year. For further information on this topic see E. J. Bickerman, *Greek and Roman Chronology*, 1968, pp. 43ff.

[4] This seems to be not quite right, since the record of the vote in the end (A. p. 83) gives 18 senatorial jurymen, 17 from the *equites*, and 16 from the *tribuni aerarii*; the option of rejecting jurymen as stated here would imply that 17 would be left from each rank.

[5] See Introduction to *pro Milone*, A. p. 47. This is not the only instance known of the circulation of a speech in revised form after the occasion of its delivery. Indeed Cicero's own *In Verrem* V (70 B.C.) is an example of a speech which was never actually delivered, but was duly published as though it had been, with adjustments to its text made necessary by events which occurred after its supposed occasion. See also the remark (A. p. 65) about the speech written by M. Brutus for a hypothetical defence of Milo.

[6] The text and the grammatical structure are not quite certain here. In my translation I have effectively adopted *existimare* in place of Clark's emendation *existimaret*; the point seems to be that the transcript is reporting speculation about Hortensius' *unspoken* motives for suggesting an inquiry.

PRO CORNELIO: NOTES

[1] Once again the text is in doubt. Clark adopts the *praenomen L.* before Domitius (following Manutius), and inserts *aliquot* (some) before *annos*, so making the

passage a reference to the year 94 B.C. On that assumption, the other consul will be C. *Coelius*, and I have adopted that spelling in my translation.

[2] Clark prints Manutius' emendation *M'.* (Manius, consul in 66 B.C.) in place of the *M.* (Marcus) in Poggio's manuscript. See, however, G. V. Sumner, *Journal of Roman Studies* 1964, pp. 41ff., who suggests *Mam.* (the consul of 77 B.C.) as a more plausible identification in the context.

[3] Not any longer.

[4] The "second" section of extracts (A. pp. 121f.) is probably not from the second speech for the defence – rather it may be a summary of cross-examinations of witnesses.

[5] See further *In toga candida* below, A. pp. 133f.

[6] See Cicero, *de haruspicum responso* 24.

[7] Text incomplete here: I have filled the gap in Clark's text with Madvig's suggested supplement *Fenestella quoque a Scipione Africano II cos.* to follow the words *ille maior dedit*, and translated the result.

[8] T. Livius (the historian Livy) was a native of Patavium (*Padova*) in northern Italy. The word *noster* (our) is usually taken to imply that Asconius too came from there.

[9] Poggio added the words *Secunda oratio* here (second speech). See above, note 4.

[10] Again, *M'.* is Manutius' emendation, and we should probably read *Mam.* Lepidus: see above, A. p. 95, with note 2.

[11] The manuscripts read *M.*, but Clark has adopted the emendation *Mam.* - a change necessary to fit the context.

IN TOGA CANDIDA: NOTES

[1] In full, C. Antonius Hybrida.

[2] That is, the Antonius who was consul in 99 B.C. and *censor* in 97.

[3] We cannot easily check these assertions; Cicero's *Account of his career* has not survived, though we know that in 59 B.C. he was thinking of writing some "Secret Memoirs" (Cicero, *Letters to Atticus*, 2.6.2). Asconius seems to be using hindsight in identifying Crassus or Caesar with the "certain *nobilis* individual", and in asserting that Crassus' *electoral support* in 64 B.C. for Catilina was

equivalent to his authorship of a *conspiracy*. The one firm allegation that Cicero is known to have made in his surviving work about events in 66/65 B.C. (apart from the extract below, A. p. 143) is the remark that on 31 December 66 Catilina carried a weapon in the forum (*In Catilinam* I.6.15). On the basis of this sort of innuendo it was readily possible for a grandiose "First Conspiracy" to be erected, especially after the actual violence of Catilina's activities in 63. The story that Cicero even defended Catilina in court in 65 (A. p. 133), which Asconius cannot bring himself to believe, does suggest an element of opportunism in Cicero's conduct which would be quite consistent with an attempt to sabotage Catilina electorally in 64.

⁴ This explanation is puzzling as it stands. If facing a charge of *repetundae* disqualified a man from candidature, then Volcacius would not need to call for discussion of the question. It seems more likely that Volcacius was instead simply exercising his authority not to accept Catilina's candidature, even though Catilina had not yet been formally charged; if actually elected, Catilina would of course be immune from prosecution until the end of his term of office (cf. Scaurus above, A. pp. 31f.). Sallustius tells us in addition that Catilina was unable to stand because he had not presented himself within the specified period.

⁵ Clark adds *non* here, and I have so translated the sentence. Perhaps after all "the *named* individuals" would be better, since they are just that.

⁶ There is an echo of this abortive episode in Sallustius, *Conspiracy of Catilina*, 18.8, dated to 5 February 65. Apart from the discrepancy of the date, it seems to bear some connection with Cicero's allegation that on one occasion Catilina carried a weapon in the forum (see above, note 3).

APPENDIX: ASCONIUS' ERRORS

This Appendix is simply a list of the main instances where Asconius seems to have made mistakes (for a really comprehensive survey see Marshall, *Historical Commentary on Asconius*, pp. 62ff.).

1. *In Pisonem*, A. p. 7: L. Cornelius Piso did not belong to the branch which called itself *Frugi*: see R. Syme, *Journal of Roman Studies* 1956, 17ff.

2. *In Pisonem*, A. p. 7: Placentia had in fact become a *municipium* by Cicero's time: see Nisbet, *In Pisonem* p. 54.

3. *Pro Milone*, A. pp. 77f.: Cicero's reference (§55) is probably to Clodius' activities in Etruria (mentioned also §§26, 50, 74, 98) rather than to the allegation that he was intending to join Catilina.

4. *Pro Milone*, A. p. 81: Cicero's allusion (§88) is not connected with Clodius' arrest at the sacrifice in 61 B.C., but to his behaviour in the 50s.

5. *In toga candida*, A. p. 129: the death of Cicero's father. According to Cicero's own statement in *Letters to Atticus* 1.6.2 his father died in 68 B.C., not 64.

6. *In toga candida*, A. p. 137: Cicero's defence of Q. Gallius almost certainly preceded this speech (see *Commentariolum petitionis* 19).

7. *In toga candida*, A. p. 139: Catilina's trial. According to Cassius Dio (38.8.1) the three groups of jurors did not cast their votes separately until a law of 59 B.C.; Asconius may therefore be simply offering guesswork in claiming to know which way they respectively voted.

GLOSSARY OF LATIN TERMS

ACTA: in this context the *Acta Senatus,* or record of the proceedings of senate meetings; the preparation and publication of this record was inaugurated by Iulius Caesar (59 B.C.: see Suetonius, *Iulius Caesar* 20).

AEDILIS: one of four annually elected officials with certain administrative duties in Rome itself (such as the supply of water); additionally, the *aediles* regularly presented, and paid for, the public Games - a useful investment for the aspiring politician.

BONI, MELIORES: the most unspecific terms of political commendation ("people I approve of"); yet they both have a noticeable tendency to be used by and about more traditionally-minded politicians; see *optimates.*

CENSOR: two members of the senate were appointed normally at five-year intervals to the function of the *CENSVRA*: their duties included the letting of state contracts, but in particular the maintenance of the register of senators, with power to admit new members and expel existing ones. After the dissolution of the office by Sulla (81 B.C.?), its re-emergence in 70 was the occasion of a notably long list of expulsions - see A. p. 40.

CIVITAS: any community of self-governing members, normally occupying the lowest grade of collective privilege. Such groups might acquire higher status in their relations with Rome, including that of *municipium* (q.v.), and become ultimately equivalent to the English derivative "city". CIVITAS also denotes *citizenship,* the status of Roman citizen: when this is the sense employed by Asconius, the word has been so translated.

COLLEGIVM: a word applied to the four "colleges" of priests (*pontifices, augures, VIIviri epulonum,* and *XVviri sacris faciundis*). However it also referred to several secular groups of people such as craftsmen (see A. p. 115); these "guilds" were probably burial and mutual benefit societies in origin, but gained significance as political organizations, especially when their suppression was reversed in 58 B.C. by

the *tribunus plebis* P. Clodius. See *OCD²* s.v. Clubs, Roman.

COLONIA: a colony dispatched abroad and composed of Roman citizens who continued to enjoy their right of suffrage as well as their own local autonomy. In Cicero's time many consisted of veteran soldiers granted holdings of land after their discharge from military service.

COMITIA CENTVRIATA: an assembly of the Roman *populus*, originally in military units called *centuries*, for the purpose of certain kinds of legislation and, in particular, the election of consuls.

------ CVRIATA: another and more ancient type of citizen assembly (*curiata*, cf. *Quirites*, Roman citizens), organized differently from the *c. centuriata*, which confirmed state appointments and installed priests. See Momigliano, *OCD²* s.v.

CONTIO: a public open-air meeting at which a harangue would be delivered to bystanders; while being loosely structured, such a meeting was governed by certain rules, and only particular persons, e.g. consuls or *tribuni plebis*, might hold one.

DECEMVIRI: A commission of ten men. There were several different such commissions, the one relevant here being the *decemviri legibus scribundis*. These were *patricius* (q.v.) men, appointed in 451 B.C. to prepare a new code of law after the suspension of the Roman constitution. They held office until the publication of the Twelve Tables in 449. See further A. Momigliano, *OCD²* s.v.

DICTATOR: the title of an official appointment at Rome, usually made at a time of crisis and for a period limited to six months, in effect embodying the powers of the two consuls. After a long lapse of disuse since 217 B.C. the title was conferred on both Sulla (81) and Iulius Caesar (44) (in their case *d. perpetuus* - not requiring renewal), and the word so began to evolve into its modern connotation.

EQVITES: originally no doubt the cavalrymen of the Roman

army; however, by Cicero's time the word had come to signify a class of men owning a minimum of 400,000 *sestertii* in capital, and which had provided jurymen for the law-courts of the republic for most of the period since 122 B.C. (but see Introduction to *Pro Cornelio*). Inasmuch as the most significant defendants were senators, the *equester ordo* had acquired a controversial political rôle as a result.

FAMILIA: this word denotes more than our word "family", and could include not only more distant relatives but also associates and faithful supporters of politicians.

INTERREX: a man appointed with this title at Rome if, for example, the annual elections had not for some reason been held on time. The *interregnum* was always of strictly limited duration - typically five days (see A. p. 67).

MAIESTAS: strictly a "lessening of the majesty of the Roman people" (*maiestas populi Romani minuta*), and conventionally translated as "treason". However, as defined in the Law of Sulla (81 B.C.?) it embraces offences such as that of leaving a province of which one was governor or engaging in warfare without senatorial permission.

MVNICIPIVM: an Italian community originally attached to Rome by a form of alliance and enjoying local self-government, but subordinated to Rome in questions of foreign policy. See Sherwin-White, *OCD*² s.v., for further details.

NOBILIS: noble, in the sense of belonging to a family whose members have reached, and preferably continue to reach, high office; normally the consulship is meant, but the term may be used more loosely.

NOVVS HOMO: a "new man" lacked ancestors who qualified as *nobilis* (q.v.), and therefore could not enjoy the advantages in politics that came from having them, e.g. a famous family name for use at election-time, and a body of loyal voters. The most obvious example of a *novus homo* is Cicero himself.

OPTIMATES: a term always carrying overtones of approval

(*optimus* = best), and normally used to refer to politicians of a strongly traditional style, by contrast with *populares* (q.v.)

PATRICIVS, PLEBEIVS: originally words denoting the historic division of the Roman people into two classes, the *patricii* occupying the positions of power, the *plebeii* being subordinate. By Cicero's time, with the "Struggle of the Orders" long past, these terms had largely lost their significance; however, the office of *tribunus plebis* was naturally confined to the *plebs*, and one of the two annual consuls had to be a *plebeius*. In 58 B.C. P. Clodius Pulcher was specially transferred to the *plebs* by legal enactment in order to be eligible for election as *tribunus* (A. p. 41). As time went on, the two terms became gradually merged into the distinction between senators and *equites* on the one hand and the remainder of the people on the other.

PERDVELLIO: an offence in criminal law similar to treason (cognate with Latin *bellum*); there was an archaic quality to it, and the trial of Roscius in 63 (see Cicero's speech *pro Roscio perduellionis reo*) had the air of a revival of ancient ritual.

POPVLARES: a flexible label for those politicians adopting an appeal to supporters outside the traditional senatorial groupings. A description of tactics and methods rather than of the content of any political programme.

POPVLVS: the Roman people, a term used variously to refer to the entire citizen body or to that portion of it that consisted of non-senators.

QVAESITOR: an investigator and president of a commission of inquiry. Originally the term was probably confined to the chairman of an extraordinary commission, but was also applied to the presiding magistrate at a regular court of law (*quaestio*). Not to be confused with the annual elective office of *quaestor*, occupied by men early in their political careers.

(RES) REPETVNDAE: technical term for a charge of mis-

government in a province, especially of extortion and embezzlement; such a charge was a hazard regularly faced at the hands of his opponents by a politician returning from a term of duty as governor abroad.

TRIBVNI AERARII: a puzzling group of persons, originally consisting, according to Varro, of army paymasters. In the first century B.C. (from 70 onwards) they evidently formed a third constituent of the jury panels, in addition to senators and *equites* (see A. pp. 23f.), having possibly a slightly lower wealth qualification. It is clear from Asconius's remarks that their votes were identified and counted separately from those of the other two groups.

TRIBVNVS PLEBIS: a tribune of the *plebs* (q.v.), an official position originally created to represent the interests of the plebs after the Struggle of the Orders, which remained open only to *plebeii* (see *patricius* above). Since the main powers of the *tribunus* were those of proposing legislation to the assembly of the *populus* and of obstructing others' legislation by the exercise of the veto, the office was a significant feature in the political conflicts of Cicero's period. See further Introduction to *Pro Cornelio*, A. p. 87.

TRIVMVIR (CAPITALIS): member of a body of three officials, responsible for executions and for the maintenance of prisons.

VICVS: "The smallest agglomeration of buildings forming a recognized unit" (Sherwin-White, *OCD*² s.v.). That is, the word regularly denotes a village; in Rome, however, the reference is to the *sub-districts* of the city, presided over by *vicomagistri* and grouped into *regiones*. These officials were abolished in 64 B.C., then reinstated, like the *collegia* (q.v.), by P. Clodius in 58 B.C. as a useful source of political power. See A. pp. 11f.

INDEX OF PROPER NAMES

Note. In a forlorn attempt at consistency, I have always indexed Roman citizens under their second name (the *nomen*), even when the third (the *cognomen*) is more familiar – so C. Sempronius Gracchus will be found under *Sempronius*; full cross-references are included in order to help the reader find the way. Page numbers refer to pages in this book; references to the text of Asconius are always to the corresponding page in the translation (i.e. the odd-numbered page). I have aimed to include the names of all persons, except Asconius and Cicero himself.

In this index, *cos. (des.)* = *consul (designate)*, *pr.* = *praetor*, *aed.* = *aedilis*, *tr.pl.* = *tribunus plebis*, *dict.* = *dictator*, *pont. max.* = *pontifex maximus*.